# The Ones We Wait For

*A Novel*

MICHAEL V. IVANOV

Copyright © 2024 Michael V. Ivanov

All rights reserved.

This book or any portion thereof

may not be reproduced or used in any manner whatsoever

without the express written permission of the publisher

except for the use of brief quotations in a book review.

ISBN-13:   979-8-9853041-7-6

For speaking inquiries, please visit Michael's website below

Special discounts are available on quantity purchases by corporations, associations, and others. For details, contact the publisher at the web address below.

www.SPEAKLIFE365.com

This book is dedicated to my readers. I hope it inspires you to imagine heaven, dear friends.

-Michael

Other books by Michael V. Ivanov

*The Mount of Olives:*
*11 Declarations to an Extraordinary Life*

*The Traveler's Secret:*
*Ancient Proverbs for Better Living*

*The Servant With One Talent:*
*Five Success Principles from the Greatest Parable Ever Told*

*The Cabin at the End of the Train:*
*A Story About Pursuing Dreams*

## Contents

        Prologue

| | | |
|---|---|---|
| One | The Doorsteps of Paradise | 1 |
| Two | Keeper of the Forest | 21 |
| Three | John's Cabin | 52 |
| Four | The Train | 70 |
| Five | The Elixir of Life | 92 |
| Six | The Pit | 109 |
| Seven | The Great Reunion | 138 |
| | God's Promises | 158 |
| | About the Author | 161 |
| | Discover more books from Michael | 163 |

# Prologue

Some of the events in this story came to me through vivid dreams that jolted me awake, compelling me to scribble them down before they faded with the night. I never planned for them to become part of a novel, but those notes sparked the idea for this story. Many other details were inspired by reading the accounts of people who had near-death experiences, people who claim to have glimpsed heaven. To my surprise, their accounts often mirrored my own dreams and imagination of what those first moments after death might be like. Still, other aspects are drawn from biblical descriptions, revelations, and the promises Jesus made about what we will see and experience when we cross into eternity.

Though *"no eye has seen, no ear has heard, and no human mind has conceived the things God has prepared for those who love him,"* this story expresses my anticipation of God's promises. It is meant to offer hope to the hopeless, peace to those who have lost loved ones, and perhaps even challenge those who believe heaven is a myth to imagine it.

I want to be clear—I have not intended to contradict anything God has promised. As you read, I ask for grace as a writer, for I am just a human being, like you, in constant wonder and awe of what awaits us on the other side. I believe that if we spent more time imagining heaven and studying the promises of what's in store for us, we might become better people while still here on Earth.

# One

## *The Doorsteps of Paradise*

Her name was Anna, and that was all I had—no family name, middle or last initials, history, or background, just a single name. For this meeting, it seemed those details weren't necessary.

The note had simply read: *Greet Anna on the platform - Afternoon train.*

I folded the note in half and slipped it into my jacket pocket. A glance at the sun told me the timing was just about right. With any luck, there wouldn't be more than one Anna on the train.

As I scanned the platform, I spotted her. Her silver hair was neatly pulled back and secured with a butterfly clip. She wore a plain black skirt, white socks with black single-buckle shoes, and a loose grey cashmere sweater draped over a white blouse with pearl buttons. Her face, free of makeup and cosmetic enhancements, bore the marks of time—thin, wrinkled, and dotted with age spots. Despite her unremarkable appearance, she had an undeniable grace about her, hinting at a beauty that had once been striking. I estimated she was around eighty years old.

I knew it was Anna because she looked lost, standing alone on the platform among a sea of disembarked passengers. The others had already been approached by their guides. She had her hands tightly clasped in front of her, her eyes darting anxiously from side to side. She seemed to be trying hard to appear composed, but I could tell she was frightened.

Leaning against the cedar plank siding of the station, I had observed her from a distance until I realized the longer she stood alone, the more it likely prolonged her distress.

My task was clear: to greet her as soon as she arrived and stay by her side for the journey. In all my time as a guide, punctuality had been my hallmark, ensuring that new arrivals were met promptly as the train came to a halt. The sudden shift in scenery was always overwhelming, even for those who arrived with expectations. No matter how much one might anticipate the experience, it never quite matches the reality. After all, there were no postcards to send from this place.

So why did I hesitate now? I had welcomed and guided countless newcomers; it was routine for me. For us guides, arrival day was meant to be exciting. Yet, I found myself unexpectedly nervous. I held my breath as I watched the woman grip the railing tightly with each careful step she took down onto the platform from the train.

*She must be someone special,* I thought.

That would explain the unexpected flutter of nerves. Here, social status meant nothing; no one soul held more worth than another. And yet, every so often, a quiet reverence would settle over me, a feeling that someone among us deserved an extraordinary level of respect. Strangely, it was always the humblest souls—the ones who had quietly served in ways few had noticed. I remembered when Carl came, an elderly black man who'd been a middle school janitor, or Vicky, who had worked at a grocery deli counter her entire life. And especially when Thanh arrived, a small, delicate man from Vietnam, whose presence seemed to carry a lifetime of quiet resilience. I never forgot those encounters.

There was something about this woman, too—a blend of importance and familiarity that radiated a comforting presence. I felt a compelling urge to be an exceptional host.

As a young boy, whenever I crashed my bicycle or fell from a tree, I would rush home to my mother to tend to my skinned knees, bruised elbows, or busted forehead. I'd cry myself to sleep in her comforting embrace. Even as an adult, I would drive to Mom's house when life dealt me its harsher blows. Her gentle yet unwavering words of wisdom always offered solace. I never needed to tell her everything; she knew exactly what to say, regardless of what was weighing on me. And I never left hungry. For those still fortunate enough to have their mothers, there's a profound sense of safety amidst life's struggles that a mother provides, no matter how old one gets. Mom will always be Mom. It's a feeling that defies description—familiarity, peace, safety, comfort... home. Yes, that's what it was: home.

This woman radiated that same quality. I was glad I had dressed well today.

I straightened my jacket, tugged at the lapels, and patted my hair—still neatly combed in place. I checked my polished shoes for scuffs, then squared my shoulders and made my way toward the elderly woman.

"Ma'am... Ma'am."

It took her a moment to spot me amidst the bustling platform. I weaved through the crowd of new arrivals and their guides, my arm still raised and sporting a smile I hoped was reassuring.

In some ways, the platform in these first chaotic moments reminded me of a hospital surgical unit. The guides were like nurses attending to patients emerging from anesthesia.

## The Ones We Wait For

I once had surgery to repair a torn ligament in my knee, an injury caused while playing a backyard football game. I drifted off as the cold white liquid flowed into my arm from the IV, and in the next instant, I awoke in recovery in fresh clothes, surrounded by nurses. It felt like the blink of an eye. Arriving at the station for the first time had a similar surreal and timeless feeling.

Dazed and disoriented, the new arrivals were greeted with soft voices and gentle touches—guides offering a comforting hand on an elbow or shoulder. This trainload brought a mix of people: children in hospital gowns clutching stuffed animals, a teenage couple in prom attire, middle-aged men and women in everything from business suits to worn street clothes, and a few in garments from distant lands. And like always, there were many elderly passengers.

As they stepped onto the elevated platform, they resembled infants rediscovering the world, their senses overwhelmed by the unfamiliar surroundings. I couldn't help but smile, recalling my own disoriented arrival not long ago.

Some looked around for their nonexistent luggage, while others bombarded their guides with questions. A few remained silent for a time, absorbing the new reality before speaking their first words in this strange world. Eventually, they all asked the same question: "What is this place?" Patient guides answered each inquiry with calm.

I waited until the train's final whistle screeched and the last of the thirty or so passenger cars rumbled out of sight before introducing myself. Anna stood beside me, her gaze following the train as it vanished behind a rolling hill blanketed in vibrant flowers. As the ear-piercing squeal of the wheels against the steel tracks faded into the distance, the air around us buzzed with a hundred overlapping conversations.

"Anna, I'm Luke. I'm your guide. I'll help you get acquainted with this place and take you to the city," I said.

Anna studied me with careful scrutiny, likely trying to determine if I was someone she should recognize. Her deep-set hazel eyes moved from mine to my vest, suit, pocket square, and tie before finally settling on the bouquet of tulips and daisies nestled among a dozen yellow and white miniature wildflowers I held in my left hand.

"Are you an angel?" she asked, her voice ringing with curiosity.

I laughed, relieved by the question. It was a perfect icebreaker.

"No, ma'am, I'm not," I replied with a grin. "But you're not the first to ask!" I opened my jacket, revealing the vest beneath. "Can you imagine those brutes in a three-piece suit? It's not quite their style."

"I can't imagine they'd be too comfortable buttoned up like this, especially with their big feet crammed into these tight shoes," I added, tapping my right heel against the planks. I hoped Anna noticed the care I'd taken to polish my dress shoes.

She gave me a shy, somewhat uneasy, but polite smile. I could tell she had a thousand questions but remained composed, letting me steer the conversation. From experience, I knew it was easier to gain our guests' trust if I took the lead.

When I first started as a guide, I misunderstood my role. I used to answer every question that popped into their minds without considering if they were even ready for the answers. I thought it would help move the journey along. Rookie mistake. Often, they'd get worked up, spiraling into a bit of a panic, especially since I was so straightforward. Calming them down afterward was a challenge, and getting them to follow me even more so.

Looking back, I realized that middle-aged men and women struggled the most upon arrival. When you're so busy trying to hold your life together, you forget it has an end. I would have expected the young to be the most caught off guard, but surprisingly, they handled the transition well. Though they often act as if they'll live forever, young people still carry uncertainties about life, reminding them of their mortality. That was a good thing.

Middle-aged folks, on the other hand, had often

outgrown their imaginations. Their beliefs, whatever they were, had hardened over time, and it takes effort to reshape something so engrained. They frequently arrived utterly unprepared. This place hadn't been on their radar; it didn't fit into their busy schedules. They were the most apprehensive, rarely showing the spark in their eyes that the children and elders had when they arrived. Busyness has a way of extinguishing faith, and this was a place that required a lot of faith.

You didn't need a trained eye to tell who had arrived unexpectedly and who had been anticipating the journey. Their faces usually gave us guides all the information we needed. They were either bug-eyed and panicked or calm and expectant. We adjusted our approach accordingly. If they were panicked, we took our time, easing them into their new environment and answering questions carefully, revealing only what they could handle. If they were calm, we concealed nothing.

My responsibility as a guide was straightforward, but it took a lot of experience to make it seem easy, especially when establishing a connection in those first crucial moments. I've had to pull people back from the train as they tried to leap back on or chase down those who ran in a panic. It was impossible to lose them—I knew this valley better than anyone—but I often kept my distance, running behind them, pleading with them to believe I meant no harm. Some would leap from the platform and dash desperately for the forest beyond the tracks. Those I didn't chase. They always reemerged from the brush after a few minutes, realizing the dense forest was impassable.

I made it a point to dress like a gentleman for every meeting. After all, it was the most important occasion of my visitor's life. The least I could do was greet them looking my best. However, every now and then, I regretted not wearing running shoes. Once, I had to climb a giant oak tree in pursuit of a frightened, overweight businessman after I told him how he ended up on the train.

I'll never know how he managed to scurry up that tree, still clutching his briefcase with one hand. He didn't seem fit enough to handle a staircase, let alone scale a tree. But after a few hours and a long conversation while sitting on a limb with our feet dangling high above the ground, I finally coaxed him down.

He definitely wasn't ready to hear that he could've jumped harmlessly from the limb to the ground far below. Getting him to calm down was challenging enough; I didn't bother explaining that gravity worked differently here.

I've since learned to let each arrival acclimate at their own pace. There's a method to a successful reception, and I've had to refine my listening skills considerably. I let their questions and reactions to my answers guide how much information they could handle at a time. Sometimes it's better to do all the talking, and sometimes it's better to listen.

Not long ago, I spent an entire evening on the platform with a man before he was ready to start down the stone pathway away from the station. To build rapport, I mirrored his body language, sitting beside him on the warm, sun-heated planks with my elbows resting on my crisscrossed knees. We remained silent until the sun set, and something about how it disappeared behind the mountains finally triggered a realization in him. He came to accept that life, like the day, eventually ends—whether we've accomplished everything we set out to, lived the way we wanted to, or run out of time. Ready or not, the sun sets on all things.

When he was convinced the train wasn't returning, we brushed off our pants and followed the torches into the night.

Others, like Anna, caught on much quicker, making my job easier.

Anna seemed fully aware that from here on out, everything would be different. She was curious, perhaps even a bit uneasy, as she should be, but she remained calm and composed—a woman of faith.

"If it makes any sense to you, ma'am, I'm just the person who will help you find your way from the station to the city. But I'd like to make a few stops along the way."

"The city?" she asked, touching my elbow, prompting me to elaborate. I caught a slight eastern European accent in her words.

"Yes, ma'am, the city beyond that mountain range," I said, pointing to the west, away from the station. "It's just a little journey. But everything and everyone you've been waiting for is there."

I could tell she was trying to make sense of what I was saying as she followed my finger, but she seemed relieved to hear there was more to this place than what she saw at the station. Perhaps a 1900s-era railway station surrounded by rolling hills and wildflowers, nestled in a valley embraced by jagged mountains—though beautiful beyond words—wasn't quite what she had anticipated. The idea of a city elsewhere seemed to ease her mind. She gave me a nod, trusting me for now.

"Fantastic!" I exclaimed, handing her the bouquet. "And here, these were hand-picked just for you."

She shyly grasped the bundle of stems with both hands. I turned toward the staircase leading off the platform but paused when I realized she wasn't following. Anna had noticed the tulips slowly shifting colors—from red to pink, then to purple, orange, and white before returning to red again.

I smiled. I knew tulips were her favorite; they'd been left for me earlier that day, along with the note about our meeting. The women always received their favorite flowers. And those who didn't have a favorite certainly did by the time they arrived. Every lady, young or old, was given a perfectly tailored arrangement. God knows it melts their hearts.

I let her admire them for a few moments. I didn't want to rush her. From the transforming flower petals to the birds thought to be extinct and the strange insects buzzing about, to the emerald-green blades of grass, the sparkling, crystalized fruit hanging from the giant trees—there was much to take in. This was no ordinary place. Even the most common things were wondrous and mysterious here, and I was pleased to see she was already catching on to that.

I was happy to give her all the time she needed.

I was amazed, however, at how she kept her thoughts to herself. There was no comment or question about the ever-changing bouquet, where exactly the train had brought her, or where everyone else had gone. Perhaps, like many, she assumed this was a dream. It's common for newcomers to believe it's just a hallucination they'll wake up from. Most people struggle to let go of everything they've ever known.

It was just Anna and me on the platform now. The others had already wandered off with their guides, each pair heading up one of the many winding stone paths that carved their way through the hillside, leading away from the valley and the train station. Those at ease walked arm in arm with their guides, while most kept a step ahead or behind. Some children had climbed onto their guides' backs for piggyback rides. I loved doing that whenever I was assigned to a child. They adapted so quickly, the children. I often wished the adults could be more like them.

"Not a bad view, huh?" I gestured toward the mountain range beyond the hillside.

"It's the most beautiful thing I've ever seen," she whispered so softly I almost missed it. "The colors, the greenery, the light... oh, it's wonderful. It's like peeking into a fairy tale." She sighed.

I nodded, gazing up at the rock formations that jutted out of the lush and sloping fields as far as the eye could see. No matter how often I saw it, I could never get enough of its splendor. Among the guides, we had a name for this place: The Doorsteps of Paradise.

"Take your time, Anna," I reminded her gently. "We're not in a hurry."

I once took a trip to Italy with a group of friends. The first leg of our journey led us to the Dolomite Alps in northern Italy, a place that quickly became my favorite memory of the trip. From the gondola ride up to the mountain peaks to the unexpected Dutch-style log cabins scattered across the hillsides and the endless expanse of snow-capped summits, I absorbed as much of the breathtaking scenery as possible during our brief stay. Walking along a ridge, you might have a grass-covered hillside perfect for a picnic on your right and a sheer thousand-foot drop—a death trap—on your left. Those mountains were both terrifying and majestic at the same time.

The Doorsteps of Paradise reminded me so much of the Dolomites that, when I first arrived, I wondered if I was somehow back in northern Italy.

Soon enough, I understood why the train had brought our guests to the Doorsteps of Paradise. Situated far from the city, a journey was required—a time to reflect, prepare, and accept things as they were. One can truly think for themselves when they are finally detached from obligations, responsibilities, opinions, expectations, influences, and desires. And when one can think for themselves, they begin to see things as they have not before. It's a shame people can't grasp that while they still have time to change things.

\*\*\*

With one hand clutching my arm and the other holding her bouquet, Anna signaled that she was ready, and we began our hike up and away from the valley. We followed the stone pathway along a steep ridge, pausing momentarily to glimpse the city far in the distance—a mere speck on the horizon. However, its radiant glow was visible even in the blinding sunlight. Anna couldn't take her eyes off it as we walked. Was she eager to reunite with someone waiting for her there?

The mountains around us were alive with movement and sound. Bees zipped from flower to flower, and the birds sang tirelessly. The breeze, though persistent, never quite whisked away the subtle fragrances of nature. We caught the sweet scents of wildflowers, the sharp freshness of pine trees, the earthy aroma of moss-covered rocks, and the lush green grass carpeting the hills. Along the way, we encountered a family of deer sipping water from a creek in the valley and a herd of mountain goats perched on the side of a cliff.

Throughout our journey, a gentle whisper seemed to fill the air as the wind slipped between rocks and over the crests of hills, carrying with it the faint echoes of distant nature. This constant, peaceful tone added to the sense of calm and timelessness, as if the valley itself was breathing softly in harmony with the land. The Doorsteps of Paradise were putting on a show for their special guest today.

After a particularly steep stretch, I noticed Anna lagging a few steps behind. "I'm sorry," she finally said, catching my frequent glances back. "If we could slow down, I'd be grateful. I'm not as fast as I used to be. I'm old, you know."

"Of course!" I responded with a reassuring chuckle, easing my pace. "We're heading to see John. He's a dear friend of mine and great at helping folks like you adjust to... well, being a bit slower."

Anna shrugged, her cheeks reddening slightly. "I don't know if anything can change. This is just how it is when you're ancient," she sighed.

I felt a dose of regret for embarrassing her. I just couldn't contain my excitement for what lay ahead. I had a knack for making untimely comments when I was eager, a quirk I carried over from the other side. When I'd asked John about my tendency to blurt things out and suggested that maybe I wasn't qualified to be a guide, he'd said that this place was full of imperfect people being made perfect. "Everything is as it should be," he'd assured me. "Just keep learning from your mistakes."

"Do you read the Bible?" I asked, nudging her gently.

"All my life," Anna replied softly, "ever since my mother read Bible stories to me at bedtime when I was a little girl."

"Excellent!" I said with enthusiasm. "My mother did that for me, too! So you'll remember the promise that those who have been crippled, maimed, blind, deaf, old, diseased, and disfigured have cherished throughout the ages."

I closed my eyes and recited the verse from memory:

*"He will take our weak mortal bodies and change them into glorious bodies like his own, using the same power with which he will bring everything under his control."*

"You don't mean to tell me that happens… here?" she asked, her eyes searching mine anxiously.

I simply grinned. Anna's hands flew to her mouth, her eyes misting over. "Oh… I want to believe. After being old for so long, it's hard to imagine that could ever change. Could it really be true?"

"It could, and it is!" I exclaimed, barely containing my excitement. "Among many things, this is the place where all ancient and often forgotten biblical promises are fulfilled!"

Whether she believed me or simply wished it were true, Anna pressed on with a newfound sense of hope. She moved faster now. Her expression was contemplative; her lips pressed together as if holding back unspoken thoughts. I could see her mind racing to piece it all together.

"This is so different from what I imagined," she finally said, her voice conveying disappointment. She touched her temple with trembling fingers as if trying to jog her memory. Then, reaching out, she gently patted my wrist.

"I had hoped the man who visited me would be

waiting for me here. I saw him, a figure in the light; he visited me in my room one night. I knew my time was near—I could feel it. You just *know*, don't you?"

She glanced at me, perhaps wondering if my experience before arriving here was anything like hers. I kept my eyes on the path ahead, giving her the space to speak.

"He comforted me. It must have been just a few days ago—or was it today? Time feels so different now. The warmth of his light, so bright and full of love... his embrace... he promised I would see him soon. Is he here somewhere? I thought he might be an angel or..."

I touched her tiny shoulder lightly, feeling a flash of sympathy for her disappointment. Yet I knew what awaited her and was confident it would far surpass her expectations.

"Anna, I understand it's not as you imagined. But soon, it will be more wonderful than you could ever dream. Trust me, you'll witness things that will take your breath away. Our journey has been carefully planned for you with a purpose far greater than you know. You'll understand soon enough."

I winked and flashed a knowing smile. "I think I know who visited you—the man in the light. He's a close friend of John's; they go *way* back. In fact, their mothers were cousins, and they were pregnant with the boys at the same time."

Her brows knitted together, and she studied me with an intense, wary gaze. I couldn't tell if she fully appreciated my cryptic hints. Her suspicion lingered, but she chose not to press the matter further, instead shifting the conversation.

"Does everyone arrive at this place when they... when they..." Her voice trailed off, stopping just short of asking what I knew she wanted to ask.

"No," I answered softly. "Some arrive at the city gates, others directly within the city, and some, like you, at the train station. I don't know all the reasons behind it yet. For now, what I do know is enough for me to guide people on their journey as I once was guided."

She fell silent for a moment, a growing worry spreading across her face. Her mouth drooped, and her lower lip quivered. Finally, she broke the silence, her voice trembling as she asked, "Why can't we go straight to the city? Is there something that would keep me from entering it? Could there be?"

"No, Anna!" I replied with unexpected firmness. I was taken aback by the intensity in my voice, but I needed to dispel all doubts right then and there. Doubts about worthiness plague us throughout our lives, but here, in this place, we confront and banish them.

I stopped abruptly, the pebbles beneath my shoes

crunching sharply against the stone pathway. Taking her weathered hands in mine, I looked her directly in the eyes. I felt the rough callouses and the chapped skin around her nails, evidence of a life not lived in ease—hands that reminded me of my mother's.

"Nothing has ever, and nothing ever will separate you from the love of God."

# Two

*Keeper of the Forest*

Our long, mostly quiet walk led us from the winding mountain trail to the forest's edge. The mountain silhouettes loomed, their jagged peaks etched sharply against the purple and red sky until the sun drifted beneath the horizon. Just before we stepped into the forest, I guided Anna's gaze back toward the distant city, and she smiled. In the dark, the city's glow now colored the horizon with a perpetual sunset, making the summits appear as if they were ablaze.

"The night is beautiful," she said with a deep exhale. "But don't they tire of the never-ending days in the city?"

"No," I replied. "They say the light dims to an ambient glow. That's when you can really see the stars and planets suspended above, seemingly close enough to touch yet impossibly distant—a majestic ceiling without height or end. And you don't even need a telescope to admire them. And the streets, decorated with millions of eternal flames, become even more alive."

The torches lining the forest path had already been lit, their flickering flames casting light on the massive redwoods. The trees seemed to stretch even taller in the glow, their trunks rising thousands of feet until they vanished into the starry night sky. They stood like skyscrapers, though I doubted these giants could ever fit within the confines of a city block.

In this forest, you could close your eyes and truly believe you were in the hull of a wooden ship. The trees never stopped creaking and groaning, and the constant hiss of the wind through the redwood needles sounded like a distant ocean. I could swear I once heard voices among those giant trees—I couldn't tell if there were people or creatures here or if the voices came from the trees themselves.

At first, the forest could be a mysterious, even frightening place for the new arrivals, especially those from urban settings like Anna. Like me, she had lived her whole life in a big city, a piece of common ground between us, as I discovered early on in our walk.

The forest creaked and whistled, rattled and croaked, clucked and peeped, flapped and thudded. It was home to countless living creatures, from coyotes to squirrels, birds to bugs. But to me, it was now familiar and peaceful.

The air had cooled, and I felt Anna's grip tighten around my arm as we entered the forest. I couldn't tell if she was cold or frightened. Her eyes darted around, suspicious of the shadows cast by the torches as we moved through the dense trees. She shivered slightly, perhaps a mix of both fear and chill. Each time an owl hooted, she jumped and squeezed my arm even tighter.

"The mind plays tricks on you in the dark, but I promise, this is the safest place in all of God's creation," I reassured her with a chuckle.

"Oh, I'm alright," she replied, embarrassed that I had noticed.

"You know, like all trees, redwoods don't stop growing as long as they live," I said. "Some redwoods back home have been growing for a thousand years, reaching heights of several hundred feet. It's pretty impressive if you ask me. It makes you wonder how old these giants are, being so massive. Even the biggest trees back home pale in comparison."

"They must be thousands of years old," Anna said, gazing up at each tree as we passed. After a moment, she turned to me with a questioning look. "When you say 'back home,' do you mean...?"

"Of course, I mean Earth," I laughed.

"Then I take it this place isn't on Earth?" she asked, and she quickly added, "It is remarkably similar in many ways and yet so other-worldly in others."

"Well…" I hesitated, unsure of where to start. In many ways, I didn't fully understand it myself. They say that once you enter the city, everything becomes clear—perhaps you even know everything. That's the rumor, anyway. As guides, we've seen, heard, and learned a great deal, but certainly not everything. Over the years, I've learned to keep things simple for the new arrivals. If I tried too hard to help them make sense of it all, I'd soon find myself out of answers.

How do I explain that my clothes don't tear or lose color after all this time? The soles of my shoes don't wear thin, no matter how many miles I walk in a day. I can fall from a tree without a bruise or a sore muscle. How do I convey that revisiting painful memories from my past fills me with a sense of peace and forgiveness here, while back home, those same thoughts left me trembling with hate and anger? There's a grace to this place that allows one to live completely free from pain.

Anna's breathlessness and shivering during our walk were merely habits, tricks of the mind. As the sun sets and the breeze picks up, she might feel colder, but she hasn't yet realized that her body remains perfectly comfortable, neither affected by cold nor hot. But soon enough, she would understand.

No, I couldn't explain it all at once. The new arrivals must experience it for themselves to understand truly. That was the purpose of this journey in many ways—it allowed for a shedding of the old self.

"Home is merely a shadow of this place, Anna," I sighed. "You'll soon see that home was just a sample, a mere taste of what we have here. We call this the Doorsteps of Paradise, while home is often referred to as God's garden—one of his best creations, though we humans have turned it into something different from its original intent.

"As for where we are now... I wouldn't spend too much time trying to guess our location. I don't know if you can. Some say it might be the place from which Adam and Eve were expelled. But I'm sure you'll know when you reach the city. Maybe you can fill me in when I join you," I added with a wink.

"You haven't been there yet? Are you not curious?" Anna wondered.

I sighed. "Oh, I'm curious about everything, ma'am. But for now, being here is enough for me. It's a gift, and I understand that. Even if not everything makes sense, I know I'm here because this is where I need to be most. Our creator knows exactly what we need and when we need it," I patted her on the shoulder.

"Sometimes that's hard to believe," she replied, her

voice trailing off. I noticed her eyes growing misty and remained silent—a lesson learned from years of guiding. After a few moments, she continued.

"So many times in my life, I prayed for one thing but received another, and it was only later that I realized I'd been given precisely what I needed. There were moments when I sought answers and received only a profound sense of peace, still without clarity. Other times, I wished for my circumstances to change, but instead, I found grace and patience while things remained as they were. And in times when I was on the brink of giving up, I was embraced by the courage to keep going. Courage I had never possessed before. For these moments, I have been deeply grateful. They were enough for me at the time. They strengthened my faith."

"But…" Anna's voice faltered, trembling with emotion. I saw the tears welling in her eyes. "There was one time, just one when I needed Him most. There was no comfort, peace, courage, or strength. Did He not know what I needed then? Did He not hear my prayers?" She looked at me, seeking answers, and I felt her pain deeply.

I could feel my own eyes stinging with unshed tears. The old woman's pain was so palpable it took my breath away. This was one aspect of the job I didn't like. As a guide, I celebrated and relived each new arrival's joyous memories, feeling their happiness as if it were my own. But I was also given the unsettling gift of experiencing their pain when it overtook them. It would twist my stomach into knots, make me light-headed, or compress my chest as if it were about to collapse. Sometimes, my hands would tremble, my knees would weaken, and I'd need to sit down. I never told them I was feeling their anguish in real time; my role was to help them release it before reaching the city. Yet, there were times I wished it were easier to bear. I imagined it was God's way of letting us guides walk a day in His shoes.

I wrapped my arms around her, pulling her close. "You were never alone, Anna," I managed to say. We moved forward awkwardly along the trail, and I found myself at a loss for words until the pain in my chest began to ease. I didn't know the specifics of what Anna had endured, but it clearly brought her immense suffering. At that moment, the details didn't matter. I focused on the crickets chirping around us. Their sound would fade as we approached, only to resume, louder, as we moved away.

"Be patient, Anna," I said at last. "Everything will make sense in time. Nothing I can say will truly ease your pain, but soon you'll have the chance to ask any question you've ever had." I wiped my nose and dried my palm on my pants.

"When I was a child, my mother had an old, wood-framed poem hanging on the wall of our house. It was called 'Footprints.' I think she bought it at a garage sale or something."

"Yes, I love that poem!" Anna interrupted, her eyes lighting up. "I had one hanging in my house, too."

I smiled. "I read that poem often. As a boy, it never struck me as anything profound, though I liked the comforting thought that God was always with me, especially because I was afraid of the dark. It helped me sleep at night. But as I grew older and came to moments where I was truly desperate, I understood the true meaning of that metaphor. In those times, when I thought it was my footprints alone in the sand, as the poem describes, that He carried me through."

"I always believed we'd be reunited with Jesus as soon as we…" She stopped abruptly, once again almost saying the word we both knew she meant. "Or is he still silent and intangible here like he was back home?" Anna said, with a touch of frustration in her voice.

"No," I replied, unable to hold back a smile. "He's no longer a mystery here."

"How's that? Where is He?" Anna asked, her voice growing louder with each word. "Have you met Him?"

"For a brief moment, yes," I replied. "But everyone who enters the city remains with Him forever."

"Why?" Anna's shock was palpable. She stopped walking and looked up at me, her eyes wide. "Why, after all this time, would you not enter the city?"

I rarely spoke about myself on these trips. The journey was meant for the new arrivals—a time for them to reflect. I usually kept my own story to myself. But with Anna, my role seemed more significant than I had first anticipated. She probed and pried, and I sensed she wouldn't let me off easily. Perhaps, I thought, there were some lessons here, even for me. *God knows. Everything is as it should be.*

"Anna, the reason is I'm waiting for someone. I left someone back home and can't leave until she's here. I want to be the first person she sees when she arrives here. We'll enter the city together. Without her unwavering faith and persistence, I wouldn't be here. I want…" The lump in my throat grew, and I struggled to swallow it.

"I want to make sure she knows her prayers weren't poured out in vain, that I am here, too."

"Well," she said, pausing to think. "Won't you meet her in the city, whoever she is? What if she's already there?"

"She's not," I replied. "I can feel that she isn't." I hesitated and then added, "Well, I was confident she wasn't until recently. To be honest, I'm not so sure anymore. I just feel like I need to wait a little while longer."

Anna took hold of my arm again and continued down the path. I could see she was trying to piece things together. When she looked up at me, her voice dropped to a near whisper.

"So, will we recognize people in the city?"

"Of course," I said. "Anyone you've ever lost is waiting for you there."

Anna released my arm, clasped her hands together, and brought them to her face as if in prayer. "Oh, the joy," she whispered, her voice trembling.

"There must be millions of people there!"

"Billions," I corrected gently.

"And there's room for them all?" she asked, her disbelief evident.

"My friend John, whom you'll meet soon, often says there's more than enough space—even for all who are yet to arrive," I began, my voice growing with excitement. "The city isn't confined to what lies within its walls. Beyond them stretch vast forests, towering mountain ranges, deep canyons, sprawling deserts, lush jungles, shimmering glaciers, winding rivers, and serene lakes. Imagine this: back on Earth, with all the places we could explore, there were still undiscovered areas after thousands of years. But this place—this realm—is so much more.

"Do you think the Creator of the universe would keep us corralled? Consider the planets hanging above us, the galaxies we glimpsed only faintly through distant lenses. What makes you think He wouldn't let us explore even beyond those?" I chuckled softly, not waiting for an answer, the possibilities spinning endlessly in my mind. "Humans like to think it's just us out here floating through the cosmos, but I have a feeling there has always been more than just our little blue planet."

"Like other worlds?" Anna asked.

"I can't say for sure, but I've heard things that make me think so. Worlds that didn't stray from the will of their creator, which stayed as they were meant to be—extensions of heaven, not burdened by the curse of the forbidden fruit. Worlds that remained a paradise."

Her eyes were fixated on the path as she followed my train of thought.

"We'll know soon enough! I guess what I'm trying to say, Anna, is that the walls don't confine the inhabitants; they are gateways to wonders that 'no eye has seen nor ear has heard.'

"I can't wait to see the city when it is time finally. John says there are tall buildings that nearly vanish into the sky, connected by bridges, spiraling staircases, and observation decks. Concert halls and grand amphitheaters echo with music, dancing, and laughter, and there are majestic forums with giant columns, fountains, golden steeples, and marble archways filling the streets. Anything good humanity has ever designed, painted, written, or invented on Earth was unconsciously inspired by heaven. After all, we were formed in the image of God—His creative spirit lives in us."

I reached down to pick up a polished lava-red pebble from the path. The little rocks were scattered over the forest trail as if they had showered down from Jupiter.

"Think about it like this," I said. "When brilliant minds throughout history, like Solomon, Socrates, or more recently, Sir Isaac Newton, Da Vinci, Tesla, Edison, Lincoln, Einstein, Mother Teresa, or the Wright brothers, credited their success to 'flashes of inspiration'—whether they came in dreams or moments of deep meditation—where do you think those ideas came from?"

I tossed the pebble up and down as I waited. Anna didn't answer. She simply smiled as she absorbed my descriptions of heaven, so I continued.

"When people experience flashes of originality, 'as if out of the ether,' they don't always realize they're connecting to the source of all creativity. That inspiration comes from somewhere. And I suspect that it comes from here."

I described how the libraries were filled with scrolls, books, and tablets from all of history and beyond, offering endless wisdom to those who seek it. And how the walls and ceilings of these magnificent buildings are adorned with scenes of divine revelations from the past, present, and future—telling God's story.

"Just imagine an entire city designed by the greatest architect, eager to impress the beneficiaries of His work."

Anna looked up, her lips curling into a smile as if she could see the ceilings I described, just as John had described them to me.

Encouraged by her wonder, I continued, "There are gardens everywhere, blooming with every imaginable type of plant, perfect for meditation, reflection, and stillness. And the best part... no weeds!" I laughed.

"Okay," she giggled, "now I'm sold."

Anna listened as I described crystal-clear fountains flowing through the gardens and trees that bear fruit in every season. Rolling meadows filled with eternally blooming flowers, where people can run, play, and experience pure harmony alongside every kind of wild animal. A seamless blend of architecture and nature, where jungle meets city in perfect unity.

"So, where does an old lady like me live in a place like that?" Anna asked, persuading me to continue.

"If you want to live in the heart of the city, grand towers line streets of gold. And the outskirts are dotted with charming cottages, farmhouses, and even mansions. I'm sure you won't have any trouble finding something that pleases you," I laughed. "What *I'm* excited to see most are the homes which are apparently built into cliffsides, with torches lighting the maze of walking bridges that connect them all."

"I lived in an apartment all my life... which at least meant that I had a roof over my head, praise God for that. But the cottages sound lovely!" She cheerfully added.

"Believe me," I chuckled, "I try to imagine it every day. John says the Babylonians, Greeks, Romans, Egyptians, or Aztecs, with all their genius creativity, couldn't build anything like it even if they had unlimited resources."

"What do people do all day?" Anna asked. "You're here spending your time with me, and there were all the other guides at the station; I even saw people picking fruit from the train... does everyone have a specific job?"

"Here, outside the walls, you'll see mostly guides. But there, people are free to choose their work. Some are gardeners for the vineyards and orchards, there are caretakers for the animals in the stables, woodworkers and builders, teachers and writers, singers and dancers, knitters, and tailors," I straightened my tie to bring her attention to the delicate stitching of my perfectly fitted suit, "and every other occupation you can imagine."

Anna was quiet for a moment before she continued to

press me. "The older I got, the more I saw that relationships are the hardest thing in life. How can people live—let alone work—in harmony here?"

I laughed. "Too true, Anna. But for starters, there's no stress about bills, debt, or 'keeping up with the Joneses,' which means no tired, burned-out people stuck in traffic jams going to or coming home from jobs they don't like. You won't see a hurried driver flipping someone 'the bird' or cutting in late for work."

"Dear God, I would hope not," Anna laughed.

"There's no judgment, gossip, or desire for someone to lift oneself over another. There are no cliques based on social status or popularity. There's no 'us versus them'—no Baptists, Catholics, Muslims, Americans, Russians, or..."

"Or atheists?" Anna cut in.

"Well..." I let out a dry, half-hearted laugh. "You can't deny the truth when you're standing face to face with Him."

I explained how relationships here differ from what they were on earth. It was a pleasant revelation for me when I first arrived. Finally, people were free to love and did not have to self-preserve.

"In the presence of absolute love, division becomes a thing of the past. Every individual becomes a member of the same body. A healthy body doesn't contradict itself. When you run, the right foot doesn't leave the left behind—it takes a step forward to propel the next leap, and so on. The entire body moves in one direction. As it was always meant to be."

"People aren't burdened by unfulfilled dreams, past mistakes, and failures... or even absent fathers. And obviously, there's no greed because what will you earn or hoard when everything is abundant? If you desire something, you simply ask, and it is given. See?" I tugged on the lapels of my suit jacket. "Better craftsmanship and material than anything you'll find in Italy. And all I did was ask."

"There's no vying for power or fame because people don't need to be governed and don't worship one another. Everybody is somebody here. There's no jealousy because no one will ever have what you can't have or be what you can't be. In the presence of the Creator, every ego abandons its host."

Anna scratched the back of her head and then patted her hair back into place. "People are goal-oriented creatures; don't they get bored if everything is free and there is nothing to achieve?"

"No! The adventurous, creative human spirit only thrives here. In fact, there's more to strive for than ever—but not in competition or advancement over others, rather in joyful pursuit of knowing God more and expressing the talents He has given us."

I took a deep breath, letting my gaze drift upward to the canopy of branches weaving a lattice above us. The memory felt distant but vivid enough to resurface.

"When I was in high school, a teacher once assigned us a paper: 'What would you do with your life if you had all the money, time, and freedom in the world?'" I paused, the weight of the memory settling over me. "I struggled with that assignment—I couldn't even permit myself to imagine the possibilities. I thought it was pointless, a complete waste of time. I even suggested she 'read the room' and stop giving us false hope with useless pipe dreams. I went to school in a poor neighborhood, and life felt small and boxed in. She tried to inspire us, but I didn't see it that way. I was a brat like that."

Anna rolled her eyes, her tone teasing. "Sounds like my boy. He was always giving his teachers a hard time. You two would've been thick as thieves."

I let out a small, hollow laugh, then lowered my voice. "If I could, I'd take those words back in a heartbeat. My teacher was right to push us, to stretch our imaginations like that. Looking back, I think it was a heaven-inspired idea—and she probably didn't even realize it."

"And what about God?" Anna brought me back to the present. Her eyes locked onto mine, searching for an answer. "Does He dwell there, in the city?"

"John can fill you in on the details when you meet him," I replied, "but I'll tell you this: in the heart of the city, there's a marble courtyard so immense it can hold the entire population when they gather. Encircling this courtyard is the grandest palace you could ever imagine—a building so vast it could contain an entire country within its walls."

"God's palace!?" she tugged on my arm, her voice anxious with anticipation.

"Yes," I replied with a smile.

"Oh," I added, not wanting to leave out my favorite part, "and there's a river—the river of the water of life. The Jordan, the Nile, and even the Euphrates can't compare. This magnificent river flows through the city's center, dividing it into two so everyone who lives there can enjoy its waters equally. Every day, people come to drink from it, to be renewed. Golden bridges span the river, connecting the city's two sides."

"It flows out from the very foundations of the palace to a tree near the city wall—a tree that bears twelve different kinds of fruit every month. The trunk splits over the river, roots reaching deep into the water, and branches hanging over the banks, allowing people to gather the fruit. Whether gathered at the palace in a multitude or alone in the quiet of a meadow, the citizens can engage in a deep, personal, and audible conversation with the Creator whenever and as often as they desire—

just as Adam and Eve once had in the garden."

My voice cracked with emotion as I spoke, revealing a desire from the depths of my own heart, something I rarely did with my guests. I held my breath, fighting back the tears that were beginning to well up. We walked in silence for some time until I was confident I could speak without crying.

"Imagine this, Anna. A best friend, a parent, or a spouse—someone who knows you well—can never fully understand your deepest and innermost thoughts. In fact, many of us have never fully understood ourselves, even in all the years we lived. But the One who made us knows us completely. He knows what makes us laugh and cry, what makes us afraid or insecure. He knows what makes us feel safe, content, and truly happy. He electrified every neuron in our brains and filled every artery of our hearts that carries our many thoughts and desires. Imagine having a conversation with the One who hung every star, spun every galaxy, and orchestrated every event in the universe, yet loves you more than anything He's ever created."

"Oh, what a day that would be!" Anna exclaimed, clasping her hands over her lips, her eyes sparkling with wonder.

"All my life," I began, my voice heavy with the weight of memory, "I carried an emptiness I could never quite fill. I don't think I was alone in that. Like many others, I believed that a certain level of success would be the answer. And because I never reached it, that emptiness lingered, like a shadow I couldn't escape."

I paused, letting the memory fade into the peace of the present. "But after I came here, it was gone—as if it had never existed. Suddenly, I was whole. I discovered the transformative power of forgiveness, what it truly feels like to be enough and worthy. Fear and worry are relics of another life, and loneliness is impossible here. Only then did I realize my deepest desire was never success or recognition. It was to be reunited with my Creator."

"Think of it like this: just as an infant's umbilical cord is snipped at birth, severing it from its source of nourishment, so too was our soul separated from its Creator at birth. We were given the chance to make it on our own, to choose for ourselves, yet the void remained because it was always the Creator's desire to be one with us again."

Anna nodded as she listened.

"But the good news is," I continued, "that the void we've carried all our lives is forever filled in the presence of the one who made us."

"Oh," Anna sighed, her voice softening. "Dear God, that truly is good news."

Again, we let the silence linger as we walked. Usually, I left the descriptions of the city to John, but lately, I'd felt a deep longing for the place. My excitement had taken over, and I found myself sharing everything I knew, though I had yet to experience it from within.

I turned to look at her. "Is there someone in particular waiting for you there, Anna?"

"Yes, there is," she replied, her gaze fixed on the towering trees. She didn't elaborate; she continued to admire the giant trees as we walked. After some time, she broke the silence.

"Who lights these torches every night?"

"The keeper of the forest," I answered. "John."

"Every night?"

"Every night."

"So you've never been inside the city walls?" she asked.

"I've only caught glimpses from the gates that lead into its outer gardens. That's where I leave the people I guide before I return here to the valley. The city is mostly hidden from sight but glows, radiating with energy and light. It draws you into it. And the singing from within… oh man, it's the most beautiful sound I've ever heard."

I paused, recalling one particular day when turning my back on the gates and returning to the valley was especially tough. It's hard to walk away from a place you know is home.

I described it to Anna. "Once, I was there just as the gates opened, and an army of horse-drawn chariots marched out. The sound of hooves on the road was like thunder—I had to cover my ears. The ground shook so violently, I thought my knees would give out."

"The riders," Anna urged, "what did they look like?"

"I was too afraid to look," I admitted, my gaze dropping to the stone pathway as I recalled that day. "But I did sneak a peek. When I caught the eye of one of the riders passing by, I thought I would turn to stone."

I swallowed hard, the mere memory of that angel tightening my throat. "He must have been at least fifteen feet tall in that chariot, towering like some mythical giant. And that gold lion's head emblem mounted on his bronze helmet? I could swear it was alive; it was enough to make anyone's knees weak. And his face looked like it had been to hell and back—probably literally. As God is my witness, I thought I was going to die a second time; his glare was sucking the life out of me. This was no Cupid-like angel, you know, the ones with little wings, a bow and arrow, and bare butt cheeks."

Anna burst out laughing, stumbling over a stone in the pathway. I caught her just in time to keep her from falling to her knees. She was thoroughly enjoying my retelling of the encounter.

"I'm glad you find my moment of trepidation

amusing," I joked. "The only thing that kept me standing was hearing a loud but not audible voice, if that makes any sense. It said, 'Do not be afraid,' but even then, I had to look down as the other chariots thundered by. I was still afraid."

"Wow," Anna whispered, her head shaking in amazement.

"Do you remember reading about when Jesus was in the Garden of Gethsemane just before his arrest?" I asked her. She nodded.

"Remember how his disciples wanted to fight the temple guards as if their skinny, malnourished arms and measly blades could have protected him? But Jesus told them that he could summon twelve legions of angels to his aid if he desired?"

"Yes!" Anna said.

"Well, I used to wonder what that would look like or if Jesus spoke metaphorically. But after seeing those chariots, let me tell you—if he meant twelve legions of angels like the ones I saw, may God have mercy on anyone who'd dare to fight them."

"Could you see anything else inside the walls?" Anna asked eagerly. "How do people move about the city?"

"John says that if people wish to be somewhere, they can simply will it, and they're there. But most of the time, you'll see them take their time—enjoying the walks, the chance encounters, and the conversations along the way. We never grow tired of that here. Especially when you stumble across someone who lived thousands of years ago on the rare occasions they are permitted to venture out of the city. Oh, the stories they can tell."

"Do you remember reading about Solomon's temple? How God conceded to King David's wish to build Him a temple, but He said it would be David's son, Solomon, who would do it since David's hands were responsible for so much bloodshed?" I asked.

"Yes, but honestly, I never quite understood all those details or why it had to be built in such a specific way," she admitted.

"Well, that's because Solomon's temple was meant to be a replica, a 'shadow' of the one in heaven. Every detail mattered. So if the temple back home was just a miniature copy, imagine what the real one here must be like."

Anna's eyes lit up.

"Think about it—one of the most beautiful structures ever built by human hands is merely a *reflection*. Try to picture how Solomon built it, with its spacious courts and magnificent entrances lined with carved cedar from the forests of Lebanon, adorned with gold and precious stones."

"And still, remember how it is written, *The God who*

*made the world and everything in it is the Lord of heaven and earth and does not live in temples built by human hands. And he is not served by human hands, as if he needed anything.'"*

"God honored the king's wishes and even provided specific instructions, but He did not need the temple. What can a man build for God?"

"I guess not much," Anna agreed.

"Yeah, it's like when a child draws a stick figure sketch of Mommy and Daddy, and her parents hang it on the fridge. God honored David's effort and filled the temple with His glory, but He is not limited to something built with human hands. The temple construction was a heroic effort, but eventually, the Romans pillaged the gold and smashed it into the dust to the point where not one brick stood upon the other. But here, His house is not made with human hands and will never be destroyed. Here, He sits on His throne, forever!"

"I can't even imagine," Anna exhaled, shaking her head in disbelief. She rubbed her brows with her fingertips. "How can someone who is supposed to be formless take on form?"

"A good question," I admitted. "Kinda hard to picture God in a physical place, right?"

"I used to wonder if everything written about life after death was just symbolic. But remember what you were taught in Sunday school? At the time of creation, God said, 'Let us make man in our image.' That means there *was* an image to replicate in the first place."

Anna seemed to be following, so I continued. "And when Jesus was comforting his closest friends, he said. *'My Father's house has many mansions; if that were not so, would I have told you that I am going there to prepare a place for you? And if I go and prepare a place for you, I will come back and take you with me so that you may also be where I am.'*

"I'm not so sure He is as formless and spirit-like here as you might think, Anna." Then I did a little pirouette before her, "Do I look like a ghost to you?"

Anna smiled. "No, you don't."

I gestured broadly at the scene around us. "What you're seeing now is the original, the true essence of what was merely a replica back home. Yes, He is out of sight to everyone on Earth, as if behind a veil, though always present. But this is His Kingdom, and it's more real than anything you've ever known!"

"Oh, so it's like one of those parallel universes?" she asked. "We read a novel about those with my ladies' book club."

"No," I replied. "Not at all. It's not a parallel universe, but the universe that has existed since before the creation of time. It's the *source* from which our world was born. Parallel universes, as theory suggests, typically operate independently of each other. What happens in one doesn't affect the other. But our world and this one are intertwined in ways you can scarcely imagine. What occurs here undoubtedly impacts what happens back home, and vice versa."

"*Nothing* that happens back home goes unnoticed here," I said, throwing my hand toward the city's light. "The city erupts in joy whenever someone back home comes to faith and their name is added to the great book of life."

Anna's face grew thoughtful, her mood shifting as if a heavy weight had settled back into her mind. "If this is paradise, the end goal, then what's the purpose of our world? Why did God create it with all its limitations, pain, and suffering? Was it a mistake? A failed experiment?" Her voice trembled with anguish. "If our world is just a shadow of this one, aren't there murders, pain, and loss here, too?"

"No!" I said abruptly, the frustration in my voice startling me. Her words cut through me, evoking a familiar ache in my chest. This question, so often asked by those new to this place, stirred a deep-seated irritation. It was a painful reminder of the age-old accusations against God—Why does He allow suffering? Why doesn't He stop the evil in the world?

But I had once grappled with these questions myself. I needed to remember that Anna had every right to ask them. Taking a deep breath, I softened my tone. "No," I said gently. "None of that exists here."

I placed my right palm on my heart, sincerely meeting her hazel eyes. "Anna, there is no more suffering here. It's all been left behind."

I considered sharing the story of how I came here, but this wasn't about me. I had found peace with my past and forgiven those involved. It wasn't God who caused the suffering.

"Anna," I continued, "what is the greatest thing you have ever loved back home?"

"My son," she answered without hesitation.

"Good," I said. "And did loving your son mean you kept him confined to shield him from all trouble and pain and from causing pain to others?"

"Of course not," she replied, shaking her head.

"But did he experience trouble and pain and cause pain to others despite your love?"

"Yes," she answered quietly.

"And did that make him a failed experiment?" I asked.

"No," she replied.

"And neither were you, I, or anyone else who has received the gift of life. Isn't it a parent's greatest joy to grant their child the freedom to explore a playground, swim in a river, play in the mud, attend school, learn, grow, create, dream, and find love? Even knowing there are risks—falls, drownings, injuries, heartbreaks, and failures?"

"Yes, I suppose you're right," Anna acknowledged. "I wanted the world for him and would have gladly died in his place."

"Indeed," I said. "And isn't that the heart of our heavenly Father? To give us the freedom to be all we can be—to create, dream, and learn what it means to love, just as He does?"

"Yes," Anna agreed with a nod.

"Would you understand love so deeply if you had never had your son?"

"No," she admitted. "I can't say that I would."

"Neither could He," I said. "Imagine this: All of creation worships Him. Jesus once said, *'If they keep quiet, the rocks will cry out in worship.'* Yet, despite the beauty of creation, something was still missing. He created light out of darkness and said, 'It is good.' He separated the oceans from dry land and said, 'It is good.' He made every living creature and said, 'It is good.' Yet none of these could understand love. So God created man and woman—beings with the capacity to love and to be loved in return. But He didn't stop there. He gave them full autonomy. He knew the risks, and still, with a heart full of love, He fashioned humanity in His image, giving them dominion over land, sea, and air. He looked at His creation and said, 'It is good.' His deepest desire was that we would love Him back, just as He first loved us."

"Unconditional love cannot exist without free will. You and I, and all of humanity, good or bad, are essential to the possibility of such love. Despite our faults, pride, and selfishness, we are still the most cherished creation in the universe."

"A failed experiment?" I said, pulling her close. "You know better than that."

"Does He love the man who killed my son?" Anna's voice trembled against my shoulder.

"Yes," I replied softly. "Just like He loved the men who killed *His* Son."

I guided Anna to a split-log bench just off the forest path, allowing her a few moments to catch her breath. She tenderly placed her bouquet on the path and settled onto the bench, resting her palms on her knees. After a few quiet moments, she beckoned me closer. As I approached, she touched my elbow and asked in a soft but resolute voice, "I'm dead, aren't I?"

"Yes," I replied softly. "In *that* world, you are dead. But here, you are more alive than you've ever been. You were in the shadow, the dream, Anna. Now you're in the light."

"I thought so," she said with a touch of resignation.

When she was ready to continue, she reached for her bouquet, only to find that the stems had already taken root, growing right there on the path where she had placed them.

"Oh… how wonderful!" she exclaimed, her eyes filled with delight.

"Yep," I said with a smile. "Nothing dies here."

# Three

## *John's Cabin*

The flickering flames led us to the porch steps of John's cabin, which fit seamlessly with the surrounding forest. Without the torches and the swarm of fireflies, one might easily pass by in the dark without ever noticing it.

Massive ferns sprawled against the porch railings, nearly reaching the overhang and camouflaging the cabin, moss-covered vines draped from tree to tree, a natural decoration over the slatted roof and stone chimney of John's cabin. Meticulously sealed with clay, log walls rested on a sturdy stone foundation. The front porch wrapped around the sides and extended to the back, where a deck jutted out over the swamp, a testament to the keeper of the forest's ingenuity.

The man was a master of craftsmanship and creativity. He'd fashioned floating walkways that linked the deck to several towering redwoods. These walkways were intertwined with staircases that spiraled upward, leading to fort-like structures nestled among the branches, hundreds of feet above the swamp below. I'd seen John's collections of thousands of books, journals, and scrolls in each of these treehouses. There were also other treehouses that I hadn't yet been invited to explore.

John's cabin attracted all the forest's inhabitants. The cheerfully deafening symphony of croaking frogs and chirping crickets filled the evening air. My old friend reveled in this natural music, and I always found solace amidst the hum of life surrounding his home.

I smelled smoke and spotted it billowing from the chimney, a familiar sight that made me smile. Whatever John was cooking up in that big boiling cauldron of his, I hoped he'd share it with us—Anna and I were starving. I gave a few sharp knocks on the thick wooden door and waited, glancing at Anna as she curiously peered around the property.

Suddenly, she gasped and grabbed my arm, squeezing between John's door and me. "There's something—or someone—there, look! A ghost!" she exclaimed, pointing with a shaky finger toward the path we had just walked.

I followed her gaze and chuckled when I saw what had startled her. As Anna described him, a tall, "ghostly" figure was leaning casually against a tree, watching us, his exposed muscular arms crossed over his chest. The ferns and wildflowers at his feet seemed to stretch toward him as if they were trying to soak up his warmth as they did from the sun. I waived at him, and the figure waived back.

"Don't worry, Anna," I assured her, "He's been there all along. Just as I was assigned to guide you today, he was assigned to watch over the both of us. Believe me, he is no harm to you."

"An angel!" Anna exclaimed. She squinted her eyes and craned her neck to get a better look. The angel's dark green eyes carried the wisdom of ages and compassion so profound it was almost overwhelming. It was as if he could simultaneously see the present moment and every moment of one's life.

His clothing, if it could be called that, seemed woven from light itself, draping around him in flowing patterns that shifted and shimmered with every stir of the breeze. There was a quiet power about him, an aura of immeasurable strength subdued by an overwhelming sense of comfort. I felt that Anna was as fascinating to him as he was to her. His gaze never left the old woman, watching her with a mix of curiosity and amusement.

"Yes, an angel," I said. "You don't typically see them in the daytime—they're somewhat camouflaged. But at night, they practically glow."

"He's just staring at me," she whispered, as if speaking

too loudly might startle the being like a wild horse or a deer in a meadow. Then, she suddenly turned and locked eyes with me. "He's not one of the ones you saw at the gates of the city, is he?"

"No," I replied, shaking my head. "You'd know if he was. The ones at the gates protect heaven from hell. They come and go but don't spend much time around humans. This one is more of a 'local,' you could say. They're a bit more accustomed to people in their land. They're always around, mostly keeping their distance. But there's nothing to fear."

Concern deepened the lines on her wrinkled face. "And what could he possibly be protecting us from here?"

Before I could answer, a loud voice boomed behind us, startling her once more as the cabin door flew open. "Everything is as it should be!"

"Everything is as it should be!" I echoed, grinning as I spread my arms wide to embrace my old friend. The warmth from the fireplace washed over us as we stepped inside, and the rich aroma of boiling spices and freshly baked bread filled the air, reminding me just how hungry I was.

"How's my favorite pretty boy doing?" John chuckled, straightening my tie with a playful grin. "Always with the suits and the perfect hair... look at him, Anna!" He grabbed my cheeks with his rough hands and turned my face toward her. "Not a single strand out of place! God could count every hair on his head, but not when it's slicked down like this." He laughed, reaching for my hair to mess it up, but I dodged his hand just in time.

"Always giving me a hard time, John," I said, shaking my head. "Some of us like to look proper for a day like this. Not everyone can pull off the caveman look!" I tugged on his camel hair tunic and beard. His beard was short and scruffy, a patchy blend of wiry and soft strands that framed his jawline unevenly, as though he'd started growing it on a whim and never quite committed to grooming it. A few stray hairs curled along his chin, giving him a rugged, slightly disheveled appearance that suited him more than it should have.

"You know, styles have changed a bit since you walked the earth, old man," I teased, knowing he had arrived here about two thousand years before me.

"In my defense," he said, raising a finger to emphasize his point, "this is how I dressed back in my day. And yes, people mocked me even then. They called me a wild man and even spread rumors about me eating locusts and wild honey." He grinned and then squatted down on his knuckles like a caveman, growling and pounding his fists into the rug. The wide floorboards vibrated with each punch, and Anna and I burst into laughter.

Just as suddenly, John stood up, his expression turning

serious. He put his hands on his hips and stared at the floor as if transported back to a forgone time and place. "I'll admit, there were more than a few times when I had to scavenge out in the desert," he murmured, his voice softer now, "and I ate whatever God sent my way. Looking stylish was the least of my worries in those days."

He seemed lost in thought for a moment, but then he snapped back to his usual loud and enthusiastic self. "When a man is put on earth to do an important job, he must do it—no matter how tough it gets, no matter what people think or say!"

"Yes," I added, "you were indeed, *The voice crying in the wilderness.*"

I glanced at Anna as I spoke, hoping to give her a clue about who John was. Her brows shot up as the realization dawned on her. When she looked at me, her mouth slightly open in awe, I winked and smiled.

"Today is an important day for our guest, John," I said, turning his attention to Anna.

"It is indeed!" John exclaimed, his eyes lighting up as he took Anna by the shoulders, kissed her on the cheek, and then gazed directly into her eyes. "We've been waiting for you, Anna."

As she stared back at him, Anna blushed, seemingly at a loss for words.

"What the world loses, heaven gains!" John continued, his voice warm with excitement. "There is so much in store for you, Anna. But first, we must eat. Come, come." He gently led her into the living room, past the stone fireplace where a steaming cauldron hung above the flames.

I followed behind, taking in the familiar yet ever-delightful surroundings of the cozy cabin. Though I had spent many eye-opening evenings here with new arrivals and had grown accustomed to the place, there was always something new to admire with every visit—a freshly built rocking chair, a hand-carved table, or a carefully woven rug.

Despite spending most of his time in the city, John obviously dedicated many hours to the cabin, putting his carpentry skills to good use. In this country, nothing died naturally, but like back home, the land's resources were given to be put to use. For every tree turned into a home, toy, or tool, another grew in its place, ensuring the cycle of life and creation continued.

The entire cabin was built around a towering redwood, its massive trunk serving as the heart of the structure and the supporting beams embedded directly into it. A staircase wound through an opening in the ceiling boards, leading to an upper room I had never ventured into but could glimpse from the living room floor. I could see shelves lining the walls, stretching from the floor to the slanted roof, filled with thousands of miniature corked glass bottles, each tinted green, purple, or blue and containing some sort of oil.

Curious, I once asked John about the bottles.

"The anointing oil," he explained, "reserved for the head of every king, president, and world leader from the beginning to the end of time. Not a drop will be unaccounted for. One day, these oils will be poured into a great bowl, and people from all nations, tribes, and tongues will witness how our leaders stewarded the great responsibilities entrusted to them. The oil will serve as either judgment or vindication, for it is they—the leaders—who kept peace among nations or plunged them into war and poverty. Everything done in the dark will be brought to light."

"Even King Herod Antipas?" I had asked, prying a bit too eagerly. John never replied, leaving the question hanging in the air. Herod Antipas was the man who ordered John to be executed.

Anna and I were seated at a small round table near the rear of the cabin. John swung the door open to the back deck and pulled the curtains aside, allowing the evening sounds of the swamp to drift in and giving us a view of the moon as it began to rise between the towering trees. He served us steaming bowls of hot stew and a buttered, salted loaf of bread fresh from his wood-fired stove. After setting everything before us, he pulled up a rocking chair and sat beside us, watching with amusement as we devoured the meal.

When we had finished, John asked how everything was.

"Heavenly!" Anna exclaimed, and we laughed. "I guess I never thought that heaven might have food."

"Wait until you get to the city, Anna," John said with a grin. "Where the food is prepared by people who know what they are doing. You'll want to cry happy tears with every meal."

As we spoke, Anna kept a close eye on John, perhaps still trying to grasp the idea that the man before her was an extraordinary figure from her faith, the very one who baptized Jesus and the one whom a desperate king had beheaded for denouncing his unlawful marriage to his niece.

Summoning her courage, Anna took a deep breath and turned to John. "John, don't tell me that you, of all people, have never entered the city!"

"Of course I have, Anna," he replied with a smile. "Unlike your guide here," he winked at me, "All my kin have already arrived. However, I come and go. Until every soul transitions from earth to heaven, work must be done. In my brief time on earth, I helped prepare people for what was coming. Here, I am privileged to prepare them for what they will enter. A different sort of baptism, you could say. My role hasn't changed. Everything is as it should be."

John leaned back in his rocking chair, thoughtfully tugging on the strands of his scraggly black beard before continuing. "You see, on earth, my task was to usher in a new age—the kingdom of heaven—where love, kindness, justice, mercy, and humility would become the new standards of living. I was sent to prepare the way for the Prince of Peace. Though I didn't live to see it fully unfold, my mission was to set the stage for that transformation. My time was 'cut short,' so to speak, but nothing was in vain."

I smiled, catching John's pun. Before meeting him, I would have never imagined that he was the kind of man who could transform even the most serious conversation into laughter. But he often did. He was full of humor; sometimes, I'd miss a joke or two if I wasn't fully present. I always struggled to see biblical figures as ordinary people. Over time, they'd turned into legends, buried in awe and myth, and people forgot they were human—just like us.

They carried fears, wrestled with insecurities, and bore their quiet struggles. The difference wasn't in their perfection but in how they allowed themselves to be used in extraordinary ways. I wish I'd understood that while I was still back home. Perhaps it would have made faith feel less distant and more... attainable.

"Here, for over two thousand years," John continued,

"I've had the joy of witnessing the fruits of that work—not because of what I did, but because of what my efforts set in motion. I will never tire of welcoming those who arrive, young and old, with the spirit of God radiating through their eyes, shining from deep within their souls."

He gazed into Anna's eyes, his voice softening as if sharing a secret. "Do you realize, Anna, that you, who lived in this age, are considered greater than even those of us whose names were celebrated and revered in the old age?"

"How could that be?" Anna shook her head, disbelief etched across her face. "How did we accomplish anything greater than you?"

"It's not about *what* you accomplished," he said gently. "It's about the time in which you lived. You walked in the light while we lived in the shadow—the age before the cross. I spent my life yearning for even a glimpse of the one who was to come and save the world. So did all the prophets before me. They pleaded with God to witness that great day. But now, even a child who knows the story of the cross has seen what the great patriarchs and prophets longed for but never witnessed: God and man, reunited."

Anna stretched her legs, crossing her ankles as she leaned back into her chair. Her fingers began to drum lightly on the armrests, an absent rhythm that hinted at the thoughts turning over in her mind as she processed the conversation.

John paused, his words hanging in the air like a revelation. "Since the time of Adam and Eve, a great separation occurred between humanity and its Creator—not because God desired it, but because of what humanity had become: prideful, greedy, murderous, envious, wrathful, lustful, gluttonous, and slothful. They ran from Him in their guilt, though He continued to pursue them."

Then he slapped his chest with his palm. "We ran from Him, not the other way around. And then we begged Him to cover our shame and nakedness, so He did. That's how the first animal was killed—to clothe us. And ever since then, our sins had to be covered by the slaying of a lamb."

He reached out, placing a hand gently on Anna's arm, his voice both tender and resolute. "Why? Because God enjoyed watching animals suffer? No! It was a foreshadowing—a reminder to humanity that our actions have consequences and of the perfect and complete sacrifice He had already prepared on our behalf."

"That's how much He wanted to get us back. But if God is perfect—and He is—and if God is just—and He is—then He couldn't simply look the other way."

John continued explaining how God couldn't ignore what man had become, just like a righteous judge can't overlook even the most minor crimes. How this didn't speak to the wrath of God but to His justice and perfection. And that's why a greater plan was always in the works. What man had broken, God was going to restore. That was the plan from the beginning.

His voice grew deeper, more intense. "Humanity accumulated a debt it could never repay. And in this trial, the judge delivered the verdict—death. But then He stood, took off His robe, and took the place of the condemned. That's you and me, Anna. He was falsely accused, bound, flogged, and nailed to a cross until He died." As he spoke, I noticed his dark eyes welling with tears.

"The Lamb was slain to pay the debts of an imperfect world, and all of you blessed souls born into that age were instantly reconciled with God—as if you had never been separated."

With that, the great man pounded his fist on the arms of the chair. "No more laws, debts, or sacrifices! Atonement was made once and for all. You didn't have to earn your way here."

"What took me a lifetime of sacrifice, self-denial, and effort was yours in one instant. Your debts—past, present, and future—had been wiped clean. We had many commandments to follow. You had *two:* to love your God and to love your neighbor as yourself. You were adopted into eternity through a great mediator—the perfect Lamb with no blemish. You were cleansed and perfect in God's eyes the very moment you believed and received the freely given gift."

Anna rubbed her temples, her voice shaking. "I don't understand it. I have never understood it. How can it be? What have I done to deserve such grace?"

"Nothing," John exclaimed, his voice filled with conviction. "That's the beauty of it! That's grace. That's love. But did it come easily? No! It came at a costly price. The Romans had a name for flogging—they called it 'The Half Death' because half of the victims died from the flogging alone before they even reached the place of crucifixion."

Anna's face twisted in pain, her complexion paling as if she might be sick. But John, caught up in the gravity of his words, didn't seem to notice and pressed on.

"The night before Jesus was arrested, he prayed in the Garden of Gethsemane, begging the Father to take away what was coming for him. He agonized so intensely that his blood vessels burst, and his sweat turned to drops of blood. Can you believe it? The Son willingly stepping under the Father's judgment, the two of them conspiring together, for you, for me."

John leaned back in his chair, his wide eyes fixed on the floor as if a dark memory was etched into its grain. Heavy with the weight of what he had shared, a long silence followed. When he finally spoke again, his voice trembled with emotion.

"What a dark day it was in heaven." He shuddered, his eyes distant. "There was weeping, and the eternal light from God himself dimmed as Jesus hung on the cross, dying. The trees here in heaven bent low to the ground, the flowers and grass fell flat, no birds sang, no footsteps echoed on the streets of gold. There was no music, no dancing. Even the angels covered their faces with their robes. All of creation hid from the agonizing sadness and pain of the Father. Nothing dared to move."

John gulped, his gaze still locked on the floorboard. The hair on his hands stood on end. Then, as if a spark ignited within him, his face lit up, and he nearly leaped from his seat. "But when he rose from the grave... oh! What joy!" His voice boomed with excitement. "Never again will there be such a dark day for all of eternity."

Anna murmured, "But down there, they're still arguing about whether or not salvation can be lost based on how one lives. It's made me question myself so often—though I refused to believe it."

"Lost?" John sighed deeply, his expression pained. "I wish they wouldn't. To take it upon themselves to be the gatekeepers of paradise—what foolishness! Can their minds even comprehend what happened on Golgotha?"

He looked at me, shaking his head in disbelief. I

shrugged. "Seems like they're better at keeping each other out of here than the enemy is," I added.

John dropped his head, his hands pulling at his black curls in frustration. "And to keep the power of the cross from another—as if it were theirs to give or withhold—may God have great mercy on those poor souls. How can one lose what one has not earned? To believe you can lose your salvation on your merit is to imply you gained it by your merit in the first place. Should we go down and ask their permission before we allow anyone to pass through the gates? Who among them is the judge? Which of them is worthy to assign tickets to heaven and hell?"

The man was practically shouting now, his voice strained with emotion. Veins stood out on his neck as he spoke, and I could only imagine the knowledge he held—the secrets of the universe, the mysteries of grace, the depth of God's love and mercy, and the necessity of the suffering on the cross.

Even though I had heard him speak about it many times, it was all beyond me. I felt overwhelmed, awash in joy and gratitude once more simply for the fact that I was here.

And for that, I had my mother to thank.

She had taught me about God. Though I never lived like a "proper Christian," I believed because the story of creation made sense. The theory that humans evolved from worms was foolish to me. Exploding stars could not have produced life; non-life cannot create life. I once debated that with my science teacher. That theory required more faith than believing everything was created purposefully and intentionally. Especially when one could simply observe nature and man's intricate, genius design. A DNA strand is a strand of code. Code doesn't just appear; it is written intentionally and purposefully. Where there is design, there must be a designer.

With all that aside, God did not ask much of us—to know Him, our creator, and to love people, His creation. But our pride and desire to be our own gods compels us to deny Him.

I didn't go to Mom's church or mingle with other believers. I was shy and perhaps a bit rough around the edges for most people. I was more comfortable in a dim corner of a pub. But I was here, and for one reason only—because of what was done on the cross.

And that was my mother's greatest gift to me… my faith.

John eventually calmed himself, sitting in silence for a long time. He mumbled something under his breath, but I couldn't make out the words. Then, leaning his rocking chair forward until he sat upright, he looked intently at Anna.

"You know, Anna, the ripple effect of your life flows

so much further than you know. What you did for the kingdom of God... let me show you!"

Suddenly, John sprang from his chair, grabbing both of us by the wrist. A blinding light engulfed us, my stomach churned, and an intense pressure pressed against my face as if we were being pulled into a vacuum at incredible speeds. When my vision cleared, I realized we had been pulled from the cabin and were now floating high above the trees, the three of us linked together by John's firm grip. Below, I could just make out the tiny wisp of smoke rising from John's chimney.

In the next instant, we were standing on the platform at the train station, just as the beam from the train's headlight rounded the bend and brought the engine to a vibrating stop. The hiss of the brakes released a thick cloud of steam that enveloped us. Anna clutched tightly to my jacket and John's wrist, still trying to comprehend what had happened. John had never done this with me before; I was just as stunned.

"In we go!" John shouted above the noise of the engine, motioning for us to board the train.

# Four

## *The Train*

Was it possible to leave heaven? I glanced back and noticed the angel a few rows behind us. He nodded, and I returned the gesture, feeling that was all the approval we needed.

The train car was empty besides the four of us. The interior lights hid the outside world, but I could feel the train gathering speed, doubling with each passing second. Anna and John sat up front, engrossed in a conversation about the times John had met Jesus on earth. When he began describing what Jesus was like here in heaven, Anna's jaw dropped—and it stayed that way.

No one was better than the wild man to get the new arrivals excited about their entrance into the city. The more enthusiastic they became, the more animated and theatrical his stories grew. He leaped onto a seat at one point, flailing his arms wildly, causing the old woman to laugh hysterically and beg him to stop.

I remembered the first time I met him. Nothing could distract him from the new arrivals when he was with them. His passion for people seemed to pour from every fiber of his being. From that first encounter, he became the older brother I never had—teasing and challenging me but mostly trying to make me laugh. This man truly loved people, perhaps making up for all his time alone in the wilderness.

When the train abruptly stopped, I noticed a sign on the wall that read "North Station." Beneath a lamppost, a clock ticked away, and I squinted through the rain to make out 1:12 a.m. Boston, Massachusetts.

As we stepped off the train, the platform was eerily empty. John grabbed our wrists again, and in an instant, we were speeding through the rain-slicked streets until we arrived in a neighborhood I recognized—South Boston.

"John, I know this place!" I exclaimed. "I used to live here!" "So did I!" Anna said, her voice just as excited. "What a coincidence." She leaned past John to catch my eye, her words hanging in the air.

South Boston was its own little universe—scrappy, resilient, a place that demanded unfiltered authenticity from anyone who walked its streets. Triple-decker homes stood shoulder to shoulder, their weathered facades battered by years of salty ocean air. Garbage hugged the curbs, not as neglect but as proof of a neighborhood that had bigger battles to fight.

By seven in the morning, the bars were already open, their doors a haven for early risers and lingering night owls seeking a sense of belonging or a brief escape. This was a place where every crack in the pavement and peeling paint strip told a story—a vivid, defiant contrast to the perfect splendor of our heavenly world.

The rain poured down around us, heavy and unrelenting. I extended my hand to catch a droplet, but it passed right through my palm, splattering on the ground. Glancing down, I realized we were standing in a large puddle gathered around a clogged storm drain, yet our feet didn't disturb the water.

"John," I asked, still feeling his firm grip on my wrist, "why are we back here?" He remained silent, his eyes fixed on a figure approaching through the rain.

A woman, partially concealed by a large umbrella, moved slowly toward us. I could just make out her skirt and rain boots beneath the shelter of the umbrella. When she was only a few feet away, she suddenly stopped, her gaze shifting to something on the sidewalk behind us. We turned to see what had captured her attention.

Two homeless men were curled beneath a makeshift cardboard shelter, propped against a chain-link fence. The cardboard had turned to mush in the relentless downpour, caving under the weight of the rain. It created a sort of spout, pouring water directly onto the soaked sleeping bags of the two miserable souls below.

"Oh, you poor boys," the woman whispered softly beneath her umbrella. Without hesitation, she set the umbrella down on the sidewalk and removed her trench coat. With her back to us, she knelt beside one of the sleeping men and carefully tucked her coat around him, shielding him from the cold. Then, with gentle hands, she tossed the cardboard aside and wedged her umbrella handle between the fence and the sleeping men, positioning it to cover their faces and shoulders.

Using the fence for support, she pulled herself up, reached into her sweater pocket, and withdrew a few crumpled bills. She tucked the money into the trench coat pocket wrapped around the first man, then turned and began to walk toward us.

I couldn't believe what I was seeing. As the old woman approached, I instinctively tried to step aside, but John's grip on my wrist held me in place. "Anna!" I called out, but she didn't look up, didn't acknowledge me at all. Instead, she passed right through us, her shoulders soaked, and disappeared into a side street.

I swung my head around to look at Anna, wondering if she had just seen herself. Tears streamed down her face, and John gently rubbed her shoulder. "That was my rent money for the month," she whispered, her voice trembling. "But I couldn't bear to see them like that."

Before I could utter another word, the air was ripped from my lungs, and a blinding flash enveloped us. Suddenly, we were standing in a hospital room.

"Oh, how wonderful!" I heard Anna exclaim from over John's shoulder. "This is the children's hospital where I used to volunteer!"

There she was again—earthly Anna—seated beside a hospital bed. A frail little girl lay there, her head bald, her eyebrows gone, and her skin tinged with a sickly yellow-green hue. Tubes protruded from her mouth and nose, connecting her to a bank of beeping and vibrating machines.

Anna gently rubbed the girl's forehead, whispering something into her ear. The three of us circled around the bed, standing behind the woman. I leaned in closer, trying to catch the soft words she was saying to the sleeping child.

She was singing—a lullaby in an Eastern European language, one I couldn't understand. I had forgotten all about languages. In heaven, we all spoke as one. But then, John's large hand gripped my wrist, giving it a sharp squeeze, and in that instant, the foreign words became clear to me.

Anna was singing an old Russian lullaby. The melody struck a deep chord within me—I knew that song and remembered the language. My mother sang it to me when she tucked me into bed as a child. We had immigrated to America from the Soviet Union when I was just two years old, but we never let go of our native tongue. At that moment, an unbearable sadness washed over me. I had not missed home once since arriving in heaven. That's the thing about our new home; words can't capture the joy and peace that embrace you when you step onto the platform. No one ever longs to return.

But standing there in that hospital room, hearing Anna's gentle voice, I missed my mother terribly. The longing was almost too much to bear. I had been waiting for her, knowing it was only a matter of time before she arrived on the platform. But I wished it could be sooner so we could walk into the city together.

I glanced around John's broad shoulders to look at Anna. The old woman was smiling, her palms pressed to her cheeks as she watched this scene from her life unfold. "Anna, I didn't know you spoke Russian," I said. "I did, too, back home. I was born—"

Before I could finish, there was another blinding flash and a sharp tug. Suddenly, we were standing amid a somber crowd, all dressed in black. Somewhere at the front, I heard a preacher offering promises about heaven, but the words felt hollow, as if he didn't even believe them. *What a dreadful eulogy,* I thought. John maneuvered us through the crowd, guiding us to the head of an open casket draped in white flowers.

I avoided looking at the dead man in the black suit, keeping my eyes fixed on a middle-aged woman seated in front of the coffin, surrounded by her friends. Though a veil hid her face, I knew it was Anna. We were at the funeral of someone she had lost much earlier in her life—perhaps her husband.

Reaching out, I gently squeezed the old woman's shoulder, trying to comfort her as she stared at her younger, grief-stricken self. The weight of her sorrow was palpable, reminding me of the pain she had carried with her all this time.

Then, we heard it—her anguished cry. "Sinok, sinok!" the Russian words for "My son, my son." The three of us stood silently, watching her shake her head beside the coffin. The words pierced the air like a knife, echoing the unbearable sorrow of loss.

Suddenly, I wanted to leave. For the first time, I understood what my own mother must have gone through when I left her behind. In my mind, Anna became my mother, mourning at my funeral. The thought made me sick. I longed to return to John's cabin and the valley, where this pain was a distant memory. But John showed no signs of urgency.

Did he need to keep us here? Was there a reason for making this poor woman relive her pain? I wanted to ask if we could go, but I didn't want to rush Anna.

I scanned the crowd at the funeral but couldn't make out any faces. It was as if they were concealed from us—visible, yet distant, like they were hundreds of yards away, though only a few feet separated us.

Then John looked at me as if he was expecting something. I waited for him to speak, but he stayed silent, his dark, piercing eyes locked on mine. I glanced at the old woman by his side and back at him. His bushy brows furrowed, and his gaze shifted from me to the man in the coffin, then back again. He was signaling for me to look.

Reluctantly, I did. The dead man was young, around my age. A bandage covered a wound on his forehead. I craned my neck to see more, and then I froze as if the blood in my veins was drained in an instant.

I tried to speak, opening my mouth, but no words came out. I wanted to move, but John's grip tightened around my wrist, holding me in place. Paralyzed, I looked up at him, searching his face for answers. He shook his head slowly, signaling for me to stay silent. It was my body lying in the coffin.

\*\*\*

It was mid-summer, and I was stuck in traffic on a sweltering 90-degree day. My old Jeep Wrangler had no air conditioning, not even a working fan, and the heat was unbearable. The day at the office had been rough—Friday, of all days, and a client at the small printing company where I worked decided to make last-minute changes to their customer files. The changes caused our programming to crash when it processed their bills, statements, and past-due notices. So the IT team stayed late, patching things up so we could finally start the weekend.

Exhausted, with tired eyes, a sweat-soaked dress shirt, and slacks clinging to my legs, I pulled into the 7-11 on West Broadway in South Boston for a cold soda. I needed something to help me keep my cool through the evening traffic. When I checked my phone, I saw a missed call from my mom. I'd call her back later.

Inside the store, I stood with the freezer doors open, letting the cool air blow over my forehead and damp armpits. That's when I heard shouting, swearing, and the cashier screaming. I abandoned the drinks and peeked around a display of potato chips, and that's when I realized I was trapped in the middle of an armed robbery.

When I saw the gleaming silver revolver pointed at the clerk's face, everything else vanished—my thoughtless clients, my sweaty pants, and the cold sodas. All I could think was that I needed to get out of there. Mom, I thought. I should call Mom. But I quickly realized how useless that idea was. How could she help in this moment?

Crouching behind the chips, I fumbled with my phone, trying to dial 911. My hands were shaking so badly that I could barely press the buttons. When the operator answered, her voice seemed to scream through the earpiece. Panic surged through me—I was sure the robber would hear. I tried to silence the phone by tucking it under my arm, but it slipped from my sweaty fingers and hit the floor with a loud thud.

The man with the gun snapped his head in my direction, shouting for me to come out from behind the aisle. My heart pounded in my ears, and my mouth was so dry I couldn't even scream. Desperately, I scanned for a back door, a way out, but there was nowhere to go.

Then he leaned around the corner, and in a split second, I lunged for the revolver. My hand clamped onto his tattooed wrist, adrenaline coursing through me. If I could just wrestle it away and throw it across the store, I could run to my Jeep and be on the road within seconds. Then I could call Mom. Everything would be fine—at least that's what flashed through my mind in those frantic moments.

But the man stepped back, jerking his hand free from my grip, and I crashed into a stand of sunglasses. "I'm sorry! I'm sorry!" I stammered repeatedly, my voice trembling. My hands shot up in surrender, but the masked man cursed, raised his revolver, and pulled the trigger.

I saw the cylinder spin and heard the hammer strike the firing pin with a sharp 'click-clack,' but the bang never came. Instead, there was a flash of light, and my head snapped back as if struck by a sledgehammer. And then... I stood up.

Only, my body didn't rise with me.

From a few feet away, I watched the robber standing over me. He hesitated and then bolted out the door. The clerk rushed to my motionless form, lying in a scatter of sunglasses. She saw the hole in my forehead and immediately retched. I tried to tell her it was okay and calm her down, but she couldn't hear me.

I stood there next to the chips, watching everything unfold—the paramedics trying to revive my body, the sheet they eventually pulled over me, the police taping off the scene. And then... I was on the train.

There were ten or fifteen people scattered around the bench seats in the train car. A gentleman in blue jeans, a checkered dress shirt, and a suit jacket slid in next to me. I could tell he was irritated by the way he kept glancing at his gold watch.

"Damn it," he muttered under his breath. "When is this thing going to get there? Who's operating this train?" He craned his neck, peering down the aisle toward the front, then looked back, searching for the conductor, but no one came to his aid. "I've got a meeting with my investors in an hour. Some of us have things to do." His heel tapped the floor rapidly.

I pretended not to hear him and stared out the window. The poor dude had no idea he was dead. I, however, had just watched my body being taken away under a sheet and understood that everything happening now was far beyond my control. Considering the circumstances, I was uncharacteristically calm. But I *was* curious—where was this train taking us?

The train sped down the tracks with such force that I found myself holding my breath, the momentum pulling me deeper into my seat. For what felt like an hour, we barreled through a long, dark tunnel, perhaps a subway. Then, suddenly, the tunnel brightened, and we burst into the light.

The sight that greeted us took my breath away. Even the busy, self-proclaimed man of importance beside me fell silent mid-sentence. This was no South Boston.

Back on Earth, I could point to a tree leaf or a freshly cut lawn and say, "This is green," or at a flower and say, "That is yellow." But now, the trees, the rolling hills, the meadows, and the flowers the train zipped past radiated with brilliance I'd never known. The colors were deep, solid, rich, and glistening as if every blade of grass and petal was infused with light. Even the bark on the trees appeared to be crystallized by a layer of diamonds.

The jagged mountains burst out of the valley floor, their stark edges contrasting beautifully with the endless sea of green and blue. They seemed impassable, like a natural fortress encircling the lush vegetation. Every detail of every rock and cliff was so clear that I spotted a couple of rams scaling a cliff miles from the tracks.

Rivers cut through the emerald valley like veins of blue, turning into foaming waterfalls and deep pools. Thousands of birds filled the air, making this entire land even more alive.

The anxious man next to me took a deep breath and sighed. A few seconds later, he reclined back in his seat, his heel finally still. Like me, most of the passengers now had their noses glued to the windows, riding in silence. Then I noticed them. Just as the train curved around a mountain bend, I saw people.

"Hey," I shouted to the others, "there are people down there in that valley!"

There were hundreds of them—men and women working and children playing and visibly enjoying themselves. The smiles never faded from their faces. The children darted between the trees, their laughter echoing through the tall grass as they chased one another around the trunks while the adults plucked fig-like fruit from the trees, dropping them into baskets. Others loaded the brimming baskets onto carts drawn by giant horses, and off they went down a wide golden road. I followed the road with my eyes until it disappeared into the distance, where a city seemed to shimmer. The radiating brightness was so intense that it was like staring into a giant mirror reflecting the sun directly at us.

As the train's whistle shrieked, announcing our presence, the people in the valley looked up, waving, cheering, and pumping their fists into the air. But there were others who didn't wave—dozens of tall, imposing figures that made the ordinary adults look like children in comparison. They stood along the road with serious expressions, wearing what appeared to be armor, their eyes constantly scanning their surroundings.

Suddenly, the blaring sound of a horn ripped through the valley, echoing off the mountains. The train vibrated, and the entire landscape seemed to freeze. A light flooded the cabin so intensely that everything around me disappeared into the glow. The train seemed suspended in mid-air, no longer moving, yet I never felt it brake. The light swallowed me whole, penetrating everything. I could see the seat beneath me through my body and the steel axles through the floorboards as the light drew closer. Nothing could be hidden from its all-encompassing radiance.

As the light approached, I instinctively threw my hands up to shield my eyes, but it was useless. Through my raised fingers, I could make out a figure at the center of the brilliance—a man now standing in the cabin before me. The light radiated from him.

"Welcome home, Luke," he said.

I didn't hear the words with my ears; they reverberated within my mind, drowning out every other thought with their undeniable authority. Instantly, I was overwhelmed by a love so powerful that I wanted to laugh and cry simultaneously. What we called "love" back home was but a shadow of this feeling. The purity of the joy that embraced me left no doubt about who this man was.

"He is the Prince of Peace," my mother had once told me during one of her bedtime Jesus stories. "He can calm a raging storm with one word."

Like an innocent man on trial who had just received a "not guilty" verdict, I crumpled to the floor with a gasp, exhaling decades of tension and anxiety in one heavy breath.

I began to weep uncontrollably, my body trembling as thirty-five years of humanity were being purged from my soul. Insecurity, anger, jealousy, guilt, loneliness, and worry—it was all leaving me. Crawling out from between the seats, I pressed my forehead to the floorboards. In the presence of this incredible and wondrous light, every dark and hidden corner of my heart was exposed, washed away by its radiance. I could feel every dormant cell in my body jolt to life, filling me with a profound peace. I had never felt more alive, real, or present than in that moment.

His hands, gentle yet heavy, cupped the back of my

neck and head. He crouched beside me, and I didn't dare look up. "I didn't have time," I cried, reaching for Him. He grasped my hand, firm, and consoling. Still, I couldn't bring myself to meet His gaze. "It got away from me," I sobbed. "Everything just went so fast. I could never get ahead. I didn't accomplish anything... I didn't do much with my life. I didn't have time. I'm sorry." I repeated the words over and over, desperate for his acceptance.

My life's goal of being well-liked, well-known, and successful was shattered in his presence. Underneath it all, I was nothing but a scared kid from South Boston.

"Luke," He interrupted my frantic pleas for sympathy. His voice was unlike any I had ever heard—if nature itself could speak, if trees, birds, animals, oceans, winds, and roaring fire could be gathered into one voice, this was the tone that would emerge.

"Luke, all those things you wanted to do and be were *your* desires. That was *your* priority, not mine. I didn't require any of those things from you. I only asked that you love others as you loved yourself. That's what was important to me."

"I didn't even love myself!" I burst out, "I'm not good enough for this place; I failed..."

"Luke!" He silenced me again, his voice now edged with a touch of sternness. Slowly, I lifted my gaze, knowing that those eyes, which seemed to contain the entirety of the universe, could see through every thought and secret I'd ever held. In this light, my life was revealed—every breathing moment from childhood to adulthood lay exposed like a single picture. But there was no judgment or condemnation or mockery—only love.

There he was before me—the meek carpenter from Galilee, the omnipotent creator of all things—and he knew my name. I was mesmerized by his presence.

"Remember, your weakness reveals my grace," he said gently. "If you believed yourself to be worthy, you would not be worthy. Be like the little children," Jesus gestured towards the window, and once again, my surroundings became focused. "They don't concern themselves with achievements or shortcomings. They see me and run to me just as they are, and in turn, I welcome them with open arms!" He smiled, and I struggled to keep the tears from streaming down my face.

"And do not worry my son," he continued. "What you couldn't achieve there, you will become here—beyond what you ever imagined. Remember, gentleness, joy, peace, patience, kindness, humility, forgiveness, and love are the things we value most here. What you did or didn't do back there won't impress or disappoint anyone here."

He covered my eyes with his hand, and a new scene unfolded. The tattooed man with the revolver reappeared, and I was back in that grim convenience store. But now, I saw what had eluded my earthly sight: the pain in his eyes, the torment of memories filled with abuse and fatherlessness, the insignificance that he felt in society. These were the forces driving his desperate actions.

I felt no fear or anger, only a deep, overwhelming sense of forgiveness. "I forgive you!" I cried out, reaching toward him. The man staggered back, dropping his gun in shock. He covered his face with his hands, and I embraced him. Just as quickly as I had reached out, my vision shifted, and I was back on the train.

"Thank you," I whispered, realizing the weight of what had happened. I understood that without forgiveness, the train would not have moved forward. Somehow, I knew that was the key.

"I must go; there are others," Jesus said gently.

"Let me come with you!" I called out, desperate.

"Not yet," he replied. "Wait for your mother. She prays for you every night. I want you to be here when she arrives. Then the two of you can come to me in the city."

"When?" I asked urgently, "Is she coming now?" The thought of my mother realizing I was never coming home was unbearable.

"Soon," Jesus said, his smile radiant. "Soon, you will be with me in paradise." With that, the light left the train, but the energy it brought lingered. I looked around and saw that everyone on the train glowed with the same brilliant light as the people in the valley below.

I wanted to stay here forever. Yet, with all my heart, I longed to go back and urge my mother to hurry. She had lived believing in this place and teaching me about Jesus. Without her stories about the cross, her boundless love, and her ceaseless prayers, I might never have found my way here.

"Forgiveness is a gift," she would say. "We can deny it; many do. But if we accept it, we are rescued for eternity."

She'd told me once about a man on death row who denied a full presidential pardon and chose to be executed for his crimes instead.

"Through His son's sacrifice on the cross, God offers us a full pardon for our crimes, but many still refuse Him."

She explained how Jesus once said, "For if you forgive other people when they sin against you, your heavenly Father will also forgive your sins."

I would wait. Jesus had told me to wait for her, and I would remain patient until she arrived.

The train jolted and began to decelerate, winding around a moss-covered cliff and into a valley carpeted with vibrant green grass and a sea of flowers in every hue imaginable. Ahead, I glimpsed an old wooden train station. People gathered on the platform, waving and leaping excitedly, eagerly anticipating our arrival.

***

I wept as I sat on one of John's hand-carved stools in the cabin, overcome with emotions. John hadn't allowed me to speak yet. My mother kept casting glances in my direction, puzzled by the sudden shift in the atmosphere. I tried to avert my eyes, focusing on the polished shoes beneath me, but she noticed the change nonetheless.

I hadn't recognized her. The last time I'd seen her, she was twenty-five years younger—but it wasn't just the years that had changed. It was as if her entire identity had been cloaked, hidden beneath a veil that only now had been lifted. How could I have missed it?

But then again, she hadn't recognized me either. Had my appearance been altered, veiled in the same mysterious way? Did I look different here than I had back home? The questions swirled in my mind, unanswered yet strangely unimportant in the face of this moment. What mattered was that Mom was here!

As citizens of heaven, we could not board the train that brought us into the valley; it was physically impossible. I had seen panicked new arrivals attempt to do so. No one could return. But John, with his unique freedom to traverse between realms in spirit, had invited me—*pulled* me along to South Boston because the day I had long awaited had finally arrived.

"You see, Anna," John's voice grew more animated, "in the end, you'll see that the greatest gift of all is love! Whether poor or rich, known or unknown, your status in the world doesn't matter here. Yes, the gifts and talents God gave you should be used to their fullest to enrich the world. But..." John rose sharply, "what you did for those men in the rain, for the children who were dying alone, for your son through your relentless sharing of the greatest story ever told—the story of our Savior—this is what truly enriches the kingdom of God! What you did for the least of these, you did for the One who made them. There are many great deeds, but none greater than these."

He spread his arms wide, inviting Mom to stand and embrace him. "Welcome home, good and faithful servant!" he proclaimed, squeezing her so tightly I feared I might hear the crack of bones.

John then sat her back down and turned to me with a broad smile, his excitement palpable. Mom's gaze shifted to me as well. He was savoring every moment of this reunion, his joy almost infectious. My heart raced, and the lump in my throat made it hard to swallow. Tears burned in my eyes once more.

"Woman, behold your son. Son, behold your mother... the one you've been waiting for." John's grin widened, revealing his delight.

"Luke!?" Mom's scream was a mix of shock and hope, her eyes darting between John and me. Her jaw dropped, and her eyes were filled with disbelief and longing. She edged toward the edge of her chair as if she might stand but remained frozen in place.

I struggled to find my voice, but no words came. All I could do was watch as the realization dawned on her face. Then, she leaped from her chair in a sudden burst of energy. I caught her mid-air. For an eighty-five-year-old, she moved with surprising agility. Her embrace nearly toppled me, but I held on with one hand while bracing myself against the table with the other. Finally, I croaked out a quiet, trembling *"Mom."*

# Five

## *The Elixir of Life*

"You waited for me… for twenty-five years?" Mom asked through her sobs. She clung to me, pulling my neck down so she could press kisses to my forehead over and over again.

"Yes, Mom, but the time here is different," I explained. "To me, it hadn't felt that long. Maybe that's why I didn't recognize you in how you showed up!"

"Yes," she replied, wiping her eyes and brushing a loose strand of silver hair behind her ears, "Look what the years have done to me."

"Well, that's because each day was like compounding weight back home," I said. "The years add up, and the bones wear down; how foolish we were to resist this place." I chuckled.

"But here, it's the opposite. It's like we grow more

alive as time passes. Our decades feel like days, and our days feel like seconds. Yet, at the same time, our seconds can feel like days, and our days stretch out like decades. And compared to ancient souls like John here…" I gave John a playful slap on the shoulder, "I'm still a fresh arrival myself."

"Even I still have much to discover!" John noted with a grin.

I hugged Mom tighter. "If people thought about heaven more, they wouldn't clutch to the fleeting seconds of life so desperately. They might live differently—love more, worry less, hug tightly, and forgive always."

Mom sighed, resting her head on my shoulder. She used to tell me about heaven; now, it was my turn to share its wonders with her. John settled into his rocking chair, gazing into the distance. Occasionally, a deep, approving "hmm" rumbled from his chest in response to something I said.

"The great King Solomon once said, 'He has planted eternity in the human heart, yet even so, people cannot fathom the work of God from beginning to end.' The human mind struggles with the unknown. We're uneasy knowing we're not in control and must live without certainty—even though certainty is exactly what Jesus promised during his time with us."

Another approving "hmm" from John.

"You know how back home, people always say, 'too much of a good thing isn't good?'" I asked. Mom nodded. "It's because the human mind can't grasp the idea of an existence without resistance—love without hate, peace without chaos, joy without sorrow. Whenever something good happened, we'd brace ourselves for the inevitable bad that would follow, believing that all good things must come to an end. But Mom, here, every good thing is just the beginning!"

With a gentle squeeze of my shoulder, she reassured me she was still listening. We remained silent, with the creak of John's rocking chair and the gentle hum of the swamp being the only sounds. Then, I remembered my conversation with Jesus on the train. "Mom, I waited because *he* told me to wait," I said softly.

"Who told you to wait... John?" she asked.

"No, Jesus! He wanted me to be the first person you saw here!" She lifted her head from my shoulder, looking up at me curiously.

"Oh! You've already met him?" Her eyes sparkled with excitement. "I wonder if it was him who stood by my bedside. He never said a word. And even with my faith, to be honest, I was terrified of dying—until he appeared. The fear vanished the moment he took my hand from the nurse and held it in his. Before I knew it, I was zipping along on the train."

"Yes, Mom, it was him! He came to me on the train. It was the best thing that ever happened to me. He knew my name and spoke to me like I was the only person he knew. And he promised we'll see him again… in the city!"

It suddenly struck me that my time as a guide was drawing to a close. Mom was here now. I wouldn't miss the valley—not even for a moment—because I knew what was coming. And though we guides waited expectantly for loved ones to arrive—friends, family, children, parents—it wasn't with the painful yearning of Earth. We didn't suffer as they did when they lost us. But it was time to go.

I wished we had understood that back home—that every season had its purpose. Every moment taught us something. Every encounter could shatter our perspective, giving us a better understanding of one another, even in heaven.

If one could live with eternity in mind, even amid the uncertainty, pain, or chaos that earthly life threw at us, there could be a place of rest… in the peace of God. It wasn't some hidden secret. It's what Jesus taught as he spoke to the desperate and weary crowd on that hilltop overlooking the Sea of Galilee. *"Come to me, all you who are weary and burdened, and I will give you rest,"* he said.

Here, we saw the purposes of God's timing and promises. Peace came with that. But on the other side, it required faith. Yet, the peace was still available. It simply required retreating inward, silencing the outside world, and reminding oneself of His promises. That's how one could access the kingdom of God.

"Everything is as it should be!" I shouted, throwing my fists into the air with all the force I could muster.

"Everything is as it should be!" John echoed, his voice booming in the night.

"Everything is as it should be," Mom repeated softly, trying to hide her smile behind her fingers. She was catching on quickly.

Just then, the night air was pierced by the whoosh of giant wings cutting through the darkness with powerful gusts. A massive bird with a wingspan of at least twenty yards made a few graceful circles over the swamp before gliding toward John's deck with incredible power. In the moonlight, we could see its razor-sharp claws unfurl and, with a solid clunk, clamp onto the raw wood of the railing, sinking like an ax into a tree trunk. The bird was like a giant eagle, but its feathers blazed with fiery purples, and its eyes were lava red. Above its eyes, broad feathers arched like eyebrows, giving it a regal, almost prehistoric appearance.

When we'd seen it before, John had explained how, in the presence of God, this magnificent creature would lower those eyebrow-like feathers to shield its eyes from God's face.

Its piercing eyes studied the three of us through the open door; suspicion etched in every glance. Its beak held a small, corked jar filled with a clear, glowing liquid. Mom stole a glance at me, her admiration for the purple bird evident in her eyes. I smiled and winked, knowing exactly what the jar contained.

John leaped to his feet and stepped out onto the deck. The bird lifted its wings as if ready to take flight, but when John spoke softly, it relaxed. He approached slowly, and the bird lowered its head, pressing its forehead against his. With a gentle nudge, it dropped the container into John's outstretched palm. Then, just as gracefully as it had arrived, the bird pushed off the railing, soaring into the night with a few powerful strokes of its massive wings. Tiny sparks, like glowing embers, showered from its feathers with each flap, extinguishing in the swamp below.

John returned to the cabin, setting the small jar on the table before disappearing into the kitchen. He re-emerged with two crystal cups and a corkscrew, grinning broadly as he held the jar delicately between his fingers, his pinky raised in exaggerated elegance. "Anna," he said, his voice full of anticipation, "it's time for an upgrade."

He set the cups on the table, removed the cork from the jar, and carefully poured the glowing liquid into each cup, the light dancing in the crystal.

"What is it?" Mom asked, her curiosity piqued.

"Living water," John replied, his voice reverent. "Scooped right from the river that runs through the heart of the city. Every day, people come to drink from it, and it nourishes everything you see here. That river flows from the throne of God."

With great care, John handed Mom one cup and me the other. His expression grew serious as he locked eyes with her, holding her gaze for a long, quiet moment.

"Anna," John began, his voice a blend of gentleness and conviction. "Since before you were in your mother's womb, God knew you. His love for us runs so deep that He humbled Himself, stepped down from His throne, and took human form to walk among His creation. Then, knowingly and willingly, died in our place, re-opening the way for us to enter this paradise, which had been sealed off. And while His body lay in the grave for three days, He descended into Hades, shattered its gates, and brought the water of life to those who had been dead since the dawn of creation so they too could step into eternity. Yet even now, some still reject Him."

John's tempo slowed as he continued, "Even the demons of hell tremble at the mention of His name, yet in their pride, they turned against Him. But fear not—hell will never overcome heaven. Twelve legions of angels stand guard to ensure that."

Mom pressed her palms to her cheeks as John spoke, her eyes closed, nodding softly in agreement.

"Jesus said, *'Whoever believes in me will have everlasting life,'*" John went on. "He was and is the water of life and offers it freely to all who thirst. *'Whoever drinks the water I give will never thirst again.'* Anna, He's lifting every burden from your shoulders, wiping away every tear, healing your scars, and gathering all your broken pieces. He's putting you back together. You will never thirst again."

With care, John lifted Mom's hands, guiding the cup to her lips. "Drink this, the elixir of life. Back home, his still, small voice guided you like a lighthouse in a dark storm, showing the way even though we were never free from the world's storms. But now, from this moment on, you will be in the light because his light will be within you. You are no longer following the beacon through the storm—the storm has passed, and all things are made new."

I knew what was coming next. It was one of my favorite experiences here. Mom and I drank the icy liquid, feeling its coldness travel from our mouths, throats, and stomachs, spreading invigorating energy throughout our bodies. My skin tingled, especially on my face. John always made me drink it whenever I visited.

"It sustains the spiritual body," he'd say with a knowing smile.

In an instant, Mom's face transformed. She looked younger than I'd ever seen her—even in my childhood memories. It was as if she'd reverted to the woman she was before I was born. She appeared to be in her late twenties or early thirties, her once-white hair now a rich golden brown. The wrinkles vanished from her face, and her whole body seemed infused with life. Her eyes sparkled with youth, framed by long lashes, and even her voice had changed—it was now full of vitality, no longer strained as it had been moments ago. I stood up slowly, awestruck by her beauty.

I leaped over a table filled with wood carving tools, hurried around John's stone fireplace, and grabbed a mirror off the wall in the living room. Giddy with excitement, I rushed back to the table where John and Mom laughed as she skipped in circles, reveling in her newfound energy.

"Mom, look!" I held the mirror up to her face. She gasped, her expression a mixture of shock and confusion. Tears streamed down her now smooth, full cheeks as she pinched her lips, let her hair down from its clip, and patted the skin around her eyes.

"It can't be, it can't be," she whispered repeatedly, shaking her head.

"It can, and it is, Mom!" I exclaimed, grinning. "We appear as we wish to be, as our truest selves. Some choose to stay young or old, just as they were before they arrived, because that was the time of life they cherished most. Grandparents often stay grandparents so their grandchildren recognize them when they arrive. I met a man who chose to keep his nub instead of having his amputated hand restored, 'It's a conversation piece,' he told me. Children remain children because that's who they are—they've always been the kids in a world of boring, overworked adults, and they sure don't want to change that here!" I laughed.

"Oh, of course, they wouldn't! Those precious little ones," Mom chuckled, her joy infectious. Then, I remembered my necklace and loosened my tie, ready to unbutton my shirt.

"Mom, look," I said, struggling to pull my necklace out from under my vest. I finally yanked it free and held it up in front of her. Two long screws were hanging from the gold chain, like trophies on display. On my first day here, I asked John if I could keep them as a reminder. I often used them as a show-and-tell piece for new arrivals, but I hadn't told Mom about them yet.

"Can you guess what these are?" I asked, watching her face closely. She studied the four-inch screws dangling from the necklace, her brows furrowed in concentration. I realized she probably wouldn't remember the x-ray from that hospital visit after my surgery.

When I was younger, I had torn the anterior cruciate ligament in my right knee during a pick-up football game with friends. During surgery, the specialist cut a long piece of muscle from my thigh and used these screws to fasten it into my femur and tibia, creating a new "ligament" so my knee could function as it was meant to.

On my first day here, when I took that first sip of John's water from the city, the screws fell out of my pant leg and clattered onto the floor. I recognized them immediately from the post-surgery x-rays the doctor had shown me. Confused, I asked John how they were still in my knee just moments before, considering that my physical body—with the screws still inside—was lying in a morgue back home.

John explained that our bodies here retained their earthly form until the water from the river of life renewed them. Just like Mom had remained a little old lady until now, even here, our bodies held onto their familiar shapes, an extension of who we were. But the moment we drank the cold, glowing water, its miraculous power began to transform us.

"It is the spirit that governs the body," John had told me. "Had you known back then that your spirit, which is one with God, holds power over your body, you could have healed yourself on command. Jesus handed that power back to us through his death on the cross. He even taught the disciples how to do it. But over the centuries, that faith has waned. As it is written, *When the Son of Man comes, will He find faith on the earth?*" I remember how John shook his head, disappointment clouding his features.

"The body, with all its fears and impulses, lived in conflict with the spirit, holding it captive, keeping it imprisoned," John continued. "Sure, you witnessed miracles on rare occasions, but not nearly to the degree you could have—what was intended for you."

"Seven hundred years before Jesus walked the streets of Jerusalem, the prophet Isaiah spoke of Him. Do you remember what he foretold about the one who was to come?"

I searched my memory, but the words eluded me. I shook my head.

"Isaiah said, *'But he was pierced for our transgressions, he was crushed for our iniquities; the punishment that brought us peace was on him, and by his wounds, we are healed.'* Even on earth, that power had already been given."

"Nevertheless!" His voice softened, and a knowing smile appeared. "Here, all ailments are wiped away."

Mom admired her reflection in the mirror; she wouldn't stop smiling. But then, she turned to me, a question clearly forming in her mind. Her brows furrowed in concentration, her eyes darting back and forth as if trying to find the right moment to speak.

"What is it, Mom?" I asked, sensing her hesitation.

"Will you take me for a run?" she asked, her voice shy but filled with a youthful eagerness.

"A run?" I repeated, surprised.

"Yes, a run! I want to feel what it's like to run again." Her fists clenched at her sides, trembling slightly as if she were trying to hold back her excitement.

I couldn't help but smile at her enthusiasm. "Yes, Mom. Let's run!"

John clapped his massive hand on my shoulder, his laughter booming. "Go on, run!"

Mom and I stepped out of the cabin, and before I could ask which way she wanted to go, she bolted off in the opposite direction from where we had come earlier that night. I sprinted to catch up, and soon, we ran side by side, her hand gripping mine.

We moved fast—at the speed of racehorses—and then even faster, closer to that of a race car on a track. Somehow, I knew we could go faster still if we wanted to. I glanced over at Mom; tears were streaming down her face, her smile wide and unrestrained. The sharp whooshes of air whistled in my ears as we passed each towering redwood.

Her hair flew wildly, whipping into her eyes and mouth, but she wouldn't slow down. I cried, too. Mom didn't have an easy life; I only made it harder as a kid. I never knew my dad. It was always just the two of us struggling through. We never went on vacations, except for the occasional beach camping trip with a few of Mom's coworkers because those didn't cost much.

Everything we owned, from furniture to clothes, came from thrift shops or garage sales. I didn't buy a new pair of sneakers until I got my job at the printing company.

After Dad left, Mom never remarried. She had no time for romantic relationships between church, work, and volunteering at the children's hospital. Right after raising me, the Church became the most important thing in her life. She always begged me to go with her, but I always refused.

I wasn't much help along the way. Anger and insecurity pretty much owned my teen years. I was always fighting—at school, in the neighborhood, anywhere I could to prove myself. I got arrested more times than I can count. Sometimes, it was for stealing from electronics stores, and other times, it was for painting graffiti on abandoned buildings. Almost weekly, I was brought home in a squad car. The local police sympathized with Mom; when they could, they'd bring me home instead of booking me.

A dad can do a lot of damage when he abandons his son.

When I turned seventeen, I finally decided to stop causing trouble. One evening, I saw her crumpled at the kitchen table, surrounded by bills and a hefty fine for something stupid I'd done. That moment changed everything. After that, my only goal was to make money and make life easier for her. But even then, I had no confidence in myself. I settled for one unskilled job after another, barely making enough to cover groceries.

Somehow, Mom managed to pay the rent and even saved enough to buy my college books. After earning my associate's degree at a community college, I landed a decent job at the printing company, but life still felt like one endless uphill climb. There were always more bills than paychecks. And then, in an instant, my time was up.

I can't imagine how much harder things became for her after I was gone. I have no idea how she managed to pay for my funeral. But none of that mattered now.

The harder we ran, the lighter my body felt. We didn't breathe hard or grow tired; instead, we seemed to gain energy with every stride. My chest throbbed with a euphoric rush, and I was intensely aware of every muscle in my body. If someone could concoct a potent blend of every possible positive emotion and inject it straight into your veins, it would only begin to replicate the overwhelming sensation I felt at that moment. I didn't know whether to cry, laugh, or shout—I did all three. Like maniacs, Mom and I tore through the forest, mile after mile, screaming and hollering. She was testing the limits of her renewed body, and it did not disappoint.

The trail led us over creek bridges, past roaring waterfalls, alongside cliffs, and through valleys. The forest was endless. We startled unsuspecting deer and birds, and as we ran, I heard a voice in my head that wasn't my own: "Everything is as it should be, my son." It was a presence that had been with me since the day I arrived on the train.

When we finally slowed down, we found ourselves in a clearing among the towering redwoods. The sun was just beginning to rise, its rays slicing through the trees, warming my skin. I glanced over at Mom—she stood with her arms outstretched, eyes closed, letting a sunbeam wash over her face. Her skin sparkled like every cell in her body had transformed into jewels.

"Mom," I interrupted her moment, "watch this." I extended my hands toward her, palms up and fingers spread wide. When she faced me, I jerked my hands up sharply as if lifting an invisible weight over my head. Instantly, she was airborne.

Mom shot up a hundred feet into the air, her initial scream of shock quickly giving way to peals of laughter. As she began to descend, I thrust my hands upward again, sending her soaring once more. When I finally set her down, we collapsed onto the dirt, lying on our backs, gazing up at the towering treetops.

I closed my eyes, feeling as though my body was expanding and contracting with each breath. It was as if every strand of DNA unraveled, only to collapse back together. My vision turned inward, simultaneously seeing myself from the inside and outside. I observed my cells vibrating and rearranging, moving to a rhythm that seemed to align with a divine design. The physical body, subject to decay and limitation, was in stark contrast to the spiritual body—an entity of boundless energy, ever-moving, ever-changing, and infinitely more alive than anything on Earth. It was a body that could transcend time, pure and everlasting, as intended before the world's corruption.

Cancer could not grow within it; its bones could not fracture; its ligaments could not tear, and no bullet could ever harm it. Perhaps this is how Jesus could descend into the grave—his earthly form battered and broken beyond recognition, torn by the agonies of the cross—and yet rise again, restored and renewed by *this* very power. It was the essence of victory over death itself, a divine transformation that defied the limits of human comprehension.

As I opened my eyes, the trees and sky morphed into a dance of shifting patterns, shapes, and colors, only to seamlessly return to their natural form. The living water sustained all of heaven in this magnificent way. Mom and I had only glimpsed a fraction of what was yet to come.

## Six

### *The Pit*

The desire to reach the city had become unbearable. I longed to run toward it with Mom by my side, to never stop until we passed through those sacred gates. But as tempting as it was, I knew my journey wasn't complete yet.

Instead, we turned our focus toward the mountains.

I inhaled deeply, my heart weighed down by the thought of what awaited us. We had one final place to visit: the pit. But I was determined to push through this last part of our journey.

It was a place I had dreaded since I first arrived. John had described the pit to me, and because I had stayed in the valley to work as a guide, I had avoided it—until now. With a sinking feeling, I realized that I had only been delaying the inevitable. Much like when I had been called to forgive the man who had sent me here, I now understood that we had to pass through the pit to enter the city.

Over time, I had watched from a distance as countless new arrivals descended with angels to the pit's edge. I had always stayed behind, waiting for them to return. And each time they came back, they changed—tears of gratitude in their eyes, kissing the ground and praising God for His mercy.

But this time, waiting above wasn't an option. Perhaps it was meant for Mom and me to face this together. The thought of stepping into that darkness now made my skin crawl.

The path led us out of the forest and up a steep cliffside, threading ridge after ridge. In the distance, the city shimmered behind two snow-capped peaks, its power like a magnetic force drawing us in.

Mom skipped along the path like a child, pausing frequently to smell flowers and marvel at a ladybug. She watched the tiny creature crawl from her palm to her wrist, its red shell gleaming. "Her wings are like rubies!" she called out, her voice filled with delight. I trailed behind her, smiling and nodding at each of her discoveries. In this new world, everyone became more like children, full of wonder, as if experiencing life for the first time.

"Are we going to the city?" she asked without looking

up, engrossed in examining something she'd picked up from the ground.

"Not just yet, Mom," I said gently. "We must make one more stop."

Her eyes met mine, sensing a shift in my tone. "What's the stop, Luke?" she asked, her curiosity piqued.

"It's the pit, Mom," I replied. "It's not exactly my favorite place here."

Mom's gaze remained fixed ahead, her tone growing more insistent. "What's in the pit?"

"To be honest," I admitted, my voice tinged with hesitation, "I'm not entirely sure. I've managed to avoid it all this time... but I'm afraid that's no longer an option."

She observed me fiddling with my tie, sensing my reluctance to explain further. Her silence urged me to continue.

"John explained that visiting the pit helps people understand why things were the way they were back home," I said.

"Let's go," she said, her voice steady, lips pressed into a determined line. I saw the flicker of questions in her eyes as she drew a deep breath, but she let them go with her exhale, keeping her resolve unshaken.

I glanced back to ensure the angel was still with us. He

trailed about twenty paces behind, his gaze fixed on Mom. At that moment, I was especially grateful for his presence.

\*\*\*

The canyon stretched before us, its layers of jagged volcanic rock laid bare as if a colossal lightning bolt had torn through the earth in a single, cataclysmic moment. It stretched for miles, a giant scar that marred the lush, vibrant landscape. The sheer magnitude of it was both awe-inspiring and terrifying. On an RV trip, I once visited the Grand Canyon, but this chasm could have swallowed it whole.

As we approached, the life around us dwindled. Ahead, a lake of dark, disturbing clouds swirled above the canyon floor, cloaking the jagged rocks, coal, and debris around the pit's entrance. The pit's depth was beyond my reckoning; even John couldn't fathom how far it descended. From our vantage point, the pit's actual size was hard to comprehend, but I told Mom that based on the few glimpses I'd had, I suspected that all of New York City could fit within the expanse of those clouds that obscured it.

The stone path curved along the canyon's edge, but we veered onto a dirt trail that descended toward the canyon floor. Mile after mile, we ventured deeper into the abyss, drawing closer to the pit. As the path zigzagged down the cliffside, the air grew cooler, and I braced myself for the inevitable stench of sulfur that would soon fill our nostrils.

When we finally reached the canyon floor, the trail led us through a barren desert, winding past towering buttes and massive boulders. We rounded a colossal rock formation, and the valley floor unfolded before us. At its center lay the lake of gloom, a swirling fog churning like a vast whirlpool over the pit.

Typically, my journey ended here, on the safe side of the path, bathed in light and at a secure distance from the pit. New arrivals continued into the fog with an angel. But I stayed close to Mom this time as the angel forged ahead, leading us deeper into the murky haze. The fog enveloped us with every step, reducing visibility to near nothingness.

The dirt beneath our feet gave way to a gravel path of fragile volcanic shale, which crunched and crumbled with each step. When we reached a staircase, the angel descended the first few steps, paused, and turned to check that we were close behind. He then vanished into the fog, his faint glow the only beacon guiding us down the damp stone steps. I glanced back and could barely make out the ridge above us.

And then I saw them: Horse-drawn chariots lined up

with thousands of drivers. They were stationed along the cliffside, their war-ready forms gazing down into the valley at us. They were the same angels I had seen at the city gates. Had they been there all along as Mom and I approached? In the daylight, their presence had gone unnoticed, but in the fog's darkness, the gleam of their armor was unmistakable. I pointed them out to Mom.

"Thank God," she whispered.

A chill prickled the back of my neck as we descended, and goosebumps crawled over my skin. Since arriving here, I hadn't felt fear, but its cold grip was unmistakable now. Fear added to the growing sense of despair I felt. Mom's fingers dug into my arm, trembling, yet her face remained resolute, a testament to the courage she had always shown. We moved in silence, each step measured and cautious. The oppressive air was stifling, filled with a nauseating mix of sulfur and decay that made every breath a struggle.

As we ventured below the cloud, our eyes gradually adjusted, revealing the distorted shadows of the landscape around us. When we glanced up, the pit and its surrounding wasteland loomed before us, a vast expanse of darkness. The distance of the canyon walls above felt like an eternity away, and I longed to escape into the light.

The gaping chasm seemed to tug at us, threatening to pull us into its endless void with each lingering gaze. We halted at the base of the stairs, but the angel signaled for us to approach the edge. He stepped onto a broad, flat rock that jutted out over the pit, a platform of sorts. Squatting down, he reached beneath the rock and emerged, gripping the end of a chain anchored to its base.

He stepped back, his back turned to us and began pulling the chain hand over hand, letting it drop to the ground in a rhythmic clatter. The heavy metal slammed against the volcanic rock, each thud reverberating beneath the cloud.

In the distance, I thought I saw dark shapes moving on all fours, darting between rocks. Were they real or mere tricks of my straining eyes? The air was filled with indistinguishable sounds—voices, wind, screams, and whispers—all mixing into a haunting whistle that seemed to emanate from the pit itself.

With a final, forceful tug, the angel heaved a mass of steaming black rags onto the platform. He seized the chain where it was shackled to the tattered pile and hoisted it with ease. The heap began to stir, revealing not just a pile of rags but a figure draped in a torn, ragged robe. The man stood with his head bowed, his face obscured. He was nearly as tall as the angel, looming over Mom and me.

"Reveal yourself!" the angel's voice boomed beneath the heavy cloud. With a forceful tug on the chain, he commanded obedience. Bony hands, pale as death, clawed their way out of the tattered rags, trembling as they gripped the edge of the hood. Slowly, the fabric fell away, unveiling a face that seemed more spirit than man. His skin was taut and ghostly pale, stretched over a skeletal frame. He was utterly bald, with neither eyebrows nor a hint of stubble. His thin, bluish lips barely seemed capable of speech, and his eyes—bottomless pits of pure black—were devoid of light or life.

I'm not sure who moved first—Mom or me—but we both stumbled backward, clinging to each other for support. My instinct screamed to flee up the steps, but the man's coal-black eyes locked onto us, and a thin, cruel smile stretched across his chapped lips.

I was frozen in place, my feet cemented to the ground, unable to tear my gaze away. The sensation was hauntingly familiar, a ghost from my past. As a child, when my Mom worked late and left me alone at home, I dreaded falling asleep before she returned because I had a recurring nightmare. I'd dream of a shadow looming at the edge of my bed, its presence paralyzing me from head to toe. It felt like the shadow pressed down on my feet, freezing me in place. I couldn't scream, turn, or even lift my head to see it. The only escape was to pray.

"Jesus, save me! Jesus, save me! Jesus, save me!" I would pray in my mind, over and over, until the terror dissipated, vanishing as suddenly as it had come.

"Hello, Anna," the man croaked, his pasty tongue flicking against his dry lips. A twisted smile curled his lips, the corners lifting almost unnaturally.

"How do you know me?" Mom's voice trembled. She released my hand, straightening herself in a valiant attempt to appear brave.

"Oh... we have a history, you and I, Annnnna."

The way he elongated her name grated on me, suggesting a past that somehow indebted her to him. I wished the angel would force this loathsome creature back into the pit, ending this encounter immediately. But it was Mom's choice to face this, not mine. This was her journey.

"I worked to give you what you truly wanted—that's all, Anna." His words oozed as he took a step closer. The smile vanished from his pale face, and his brow-less eyes widened like a cobra poised to strike, fixated on Mom with a predatory intensity.

"But you broke our little agreement," he snarled.

The angel yanked sharply on the chain, and with a powerful, decisive movement, he thrust his other hand into the man's thin neck, his fingers digging in with ruthless force. The man let out a blood-curdling scream as he dropped to his knees, his head jerking back under the crushing grip. I feared his fragile neck might snap at any moment.

"You will make no accusations here, fool!" the angel

roared, his voice echoing with authority. He slammed his sandaled foot against the man's calf, wrenching the chain and lifting his arm high above his head. The prisoner remained on his knees, stretched taut between the angel's foot and the chain, struggling in vain against the relentless pressure.

"What agreement? I've never spoken to you before. I don't know you!" Mom's voice was a mix of defiance and desperation.

"Oh, you know me very well," he wheezed, straining against the chain. "But then you betrayed me for the Son of God in that wretched little church."

"You mean Friends of Christ Church?" Mom probed, "How do you know about it?"

The man ignored her. "I could have given you a glamorous life, but all he gave you was misery and solitude. And how did that work out for you? No one remembers you now that you're gone. Where is your legacy?"

The pale man's lips twisted into a sneer, and drool dripped from the corner of his mouth.

"When did I ever pledge allegiance to you? I swear, I've never known you!" Mom's voice cracked with emotion, nearly in tears.

The angel tightened his grip on the chain and turned

his gaze to Mom. "His tongue is dripping with deception, Anna. He serves the father of lies. He is the voice you have overcome."

"Ha!" The man's shrill laugh echoed off the rocks. "I only wanted you to have a little fun. Why worship God when you could be a god yourself? That's all I wanted you to see. He asked you to serve others, but I could have made you a queen to be served! All you had to do was keep eating from the feast I prepared, and you would have been satisfied. I could have taught you to command worship, to make people kneel before you and sleep at your feet like dogs. But you stopped listening. I could have made you the envy of all women and the desire of all men, but instead, you chose to remain a peasant."

"I never wanted *anything* like that!" Mom protested.

He spat on the ground, his face contorted with disgust. "You don't know what you want! I was going to give you everything! How many times did I tell you to rid yourself of that child? You lived just two blocks from the clinic!" His gaze turned to me, and I felt a shiver. The hatred in his eyes was palpable.

"He ruined everything!" the man shrieked, jabbing a bony finger at me. "Because of him, all those fools from that pathetic little church pitied you and conspired to help you through your pregnancy. And then, like a traitor, you befriended them and left me." Spit flew from his crooked, yellowed teeth as he hurled his accusations.

"Those were my friends," Mom said, her voice trembling. For a moment, I thought she might cry.

"His sole mission is to kill, steal, and destroy Anna," the angel warned. "His ways lead only to death. He whispers war into the ears of leaders, hate into the ears of nations, confusion into the ears of the youth, fear into the ears of the innocent, greed into the ears of the wealthy, envy into the ears of the unfortunate, lust into the ears of young men, and insecurity into the ears of young women. He can smell confidence from across the world and rushes with his minions to sow seeds of doubt…"

"Ha! Perhaps you'll let me speak for myself?" the man snarled at the angel.

"Your lies have no power here," the angel replied without looking down at him.

"Love, compassion, and empathy are his enemies." The angel continued to speak to Mom. "The unity between husband and wife is like vomit in his throat, the innocence of children makes his blood boil, peace among neighbors is a thorn in his side, gentleness, and patience are curses in his mouth, a smile blinds his eyes, and love shatters his spine. Since Calvary, he has been squirming like a scorpion under a boot. On that day, he lost his grasp on humanity. His anthem now is distraction, confusion, greed, and fear. But there is another voice that people can hear if they choose to listen, and that is his greatest threat."

"It's love, isn't it?" said Mom.

"That's it," the angel nodded. "And that's why his voice has grown louder through the ages. He knows his day of judgment is approaching. He works to strip people of their gifts and talents through fear and complacency, distract them from nature so they don't see God's hand, and divide them through pride and ignorance. As the love that binds them unravels, humankind is plunged further into chaos, purposelessness, emptiness, and hate. His army is determined to sever the connection between God and people and the joy He intended for them. Divide and conquer—that has always been his strategy. That's why hell groans and heaven rejoices when another of God's children hears the voice of truth."

Mom seemed to draw strength from the angel's defense of her, taking a resolute step toward the man. I reached out to steady her, but she brushed my hand aside.

"What about this feast you claim to have prepared for your followers? Do you say I once dined at this table? What power do you have over God's creation? Human souls aren't yours to claim!" she demanded.

"They *are* mine!" the vile man shrieked, his eyes blazing with hatred. "All mine! They ate off my table; I own them." A grotesque grin spread across his face.

"God made a mistake, and we decided to teach Him a lesson," he continued with a sneer. "Long before you were ever a thought in His mind, He cast us out of the city and its gardens. But we found a new place we could rule, your little earth." He cackled, his laughter echoing through the gloom.

"Then he got the brilliant little idea to expand heaven, and we just couldn't let that happen. Especially when we saw how much He admired you. We'd lose everything. He hoped you would worship Him and return His love, and He would hand over the keys to paradise! 'Free will,' He called it," the man chuckled.

"But we weren't interested in sharing, you see?" He shook his head, laughter bubbling uncontrollably.

"It was far too easy to lead you astray, even back in the garden. We've been doing it ever since! We found a way to diminish His kingdom through His weakest link."

Mom stepped back, her movements slow and deliberate, until she was close enough to grasp my hand. Her fingers wrapped around mine tightly. Yet her gaze never wavered; her eyes remained locked on the man, unblinking and resolute.

"Can you believe it? He expected you to be servants instead of kings with the freedom to live however you wished. How foolish! Now, the more of you I can lure to our table, the more *our* kingdom will thrive instead of His. And my food? It's delicious. I'm the greatest chef to have ever lived!" He howled with glee, relishing his own twisted sense of triumph.

"I simply give them a little taste, and then they crave it," he said with a crooked smile. "Pride, envy, anger, lust, gluttony, greed, laziness—my menu has no limits. However, my specialty is pride, or 'the ego,' as you call it. That's my best recipe! Once they taste it, their hunger becomes insatiable. And the more they feed it, the less room they have for what He has to offer. His food is hard to digest; that's His fault. Love, mercy, forgiveness, what was He thinking? Those require an acquired taste. Humans don't have the stomach for that! That's why they become *my* lifelong customers. They're like cattle marching to the slaughterhouse, never realizing they're walking straight into their doom." Spit flew from his mouth as he snarled.

Mom wiped tears from her cheeks with shaking hands, pressing them to her blouse. I wanted to beg her to stop engaging with him. It seemed like he thrived on her suffering, deriving pleasure from the distress he caused her. The more she cried, the more he relished her pain, savoring every moment.

"The love you withheld from your parents in your teens," the man sneered, "just because they wouldn't let you do as you pleased—that was my trick. I taught you that. I showed you how to wield your affection to manipulate people. The gossip you devoured and spread like a plague was a dish from my feast. The conflicts with your husband, the resentments among your friends, every jealous thought, every moment of fear that stopped you from pursuing your pathetic little dreams or speaking the truth—that was my design. I nurtured all that within you… but then you stopped consuming."

His delight vanished abruptly as if he only now realized she was no longer under his dominion. His fingers clawed at the shale on the ground, crushing the fragments into dust with an expression of raw anger.

"That's because he rescued me!" Mom's voice rang out defiantly. "Once I experienced His love, I understood what a wretch I was. He is the only one who can truly satisfy. You offer nothing but pain!"

"But you belong to me!" His voice rose to a shrill, eerie cry, like the wail of a mountain lion. He lunged at Mom, but the angel slammed him back down as if tossing a rag.

The man struggled to rise from the ground, his knees now smeared with blood, black as oil. He gasped for breath, momentarily appearing defeated. Yet, a bone-chilling smile slowly crept across his face, revealing a cruel satisfaction.

"Nevertheless," he croaked, his voice dropping to a sinister whisper, "I had my fun with your little family."

Mom's eyes narrowed. "What do you mean by that?"

"Because you turned away from my voice," he

sneered, "I found new allies. We persuaded that spineless husband of yours to abandon you, fearing he might catch your so-called 'divine infection.' We couldn't have you, but we couldn't risk losing him too. And since we couldn't break your praying habit, we had to salvage what we could."

Mom took a step back, shrinking into my arms. I clung to her, bracing for what was to come. The man's fierce and unrelenting gaze bore into her from beneath his sunken brows.

"My real stroke of luck came when one of my followers stumbled upon your bastard son," he sneered. "Ah, the magic of desperation—perfect for my schemes."

His skeletal finger jabbed toward me. "He walked into the store we'd been monitoring for weeks, and I found my chance to settle the score!"

A maniacal laugh erupted from him, growing louder and more unsettling. His face twisted and contorted until it morphed into that of the 7-Eleven robber. In his hand was the very same silver and black revolver. Before I could react, he leveled the gun at me and pulled the trigger. A sharp crack pierced the air, and the flash from the barrel lit up the dark clouds above like a jagged lightning bolt.

"My son!"

Mom screamed and collapsed onto the rocks, her face

pressed against the ground. But the angel's voice thundered over her cries, "Anna, do not be afraid!"

When she saw that I was unharmed, she sprang to her feet and enveloped me in a tearful embrace. "Everything is as it should be, Mom," I sobbed with her, "Everything is as it should be!"

The angel drew his sword, positioning it against the man's throat. The man's laughter persisted, his face twisting back to its grotesque form.

"You are worthless, worthless!" he howled at Mom. "You don't belong here—you belong to me! Mine, you're mine! This Jesus, he stole what was rightfully mine! He didn't judge you fairly... if he had, you would be with me!"

Mom lifted her head from my shoulder, wiping away her tears. "Can we please leave?" she pleaded with the angel. "I've heard enough."

"Of course, Anna," the angel replied gently. He seized the man by the collar of his ragged robe and, with a powerful twist of his hips, hurled him into the pit. The man's piercing screams echoed as they faded into the abyss.

The angel raised his sword above his head and brought it crashing down onto the chain with a shower of sparks, cleaving it in two. The severed chain clattered loudly as it unraveled and was pulled into the pit. Silence fell over the pit once more as the last glimmers of metal vanished over the edge.

***

As we emerged from the chasm, the angel no longer kept his distance. Mom bombarded him with questions about the man in the pit.

"Did he really convince my husband to leave us? Was he really behind Luke's murder? Are any of his claims true? Who does he influence? Is everyone fair game? Even children? And when exactly does he gain or lose power over people?" Her questions came in rapid succession.

"Physically, he has no power over any human. He only controls those who submit to him," the angel explained. "Yet, even they can break free at any moment. Every person knows when they are doing wrong against another. You don't have to believe in God to know that your actions or words cause hurt to others. So then, if you consciously continue to do the wrong, you imitate the enemy—doesn't that make you his follower?"

"I guess so," Mom acknowledged.

"Even those who are convinced Jesus isn't the son of God, that his story was fabricated, in their heart of hearts, still know that everything Jesus taught was the truth."

"Jesus said, *If a man even looks at a woman with lust, he has committed adultery with her in his heart.*' So even those who believe they are 'good people' just because they don't act on their impulse are sinning against another one of God's children. There are no gray lines with God. You may not express your hate to someone, but when you hate them in your heart, you are doing wrong against them and even harming your own heart. Thus, the enemy continues to hold his power over you."

"Then *who* can be saved!?" Mom cried out. "Doesn't that mean the man in the pit is right? That we all belong to him!?"

"How quickly you forget about the cross, Anna." The angel gently patted her back. "Consider why he was so angry with you. It's those the enemy has *lost* that he accuses the most. The moment one repents—which simply means acknowledging their wrongdoing and turning away from it—they are released from his grasp."

"And at what point does someone run out of chances to repent?" she challenged him.

The angel chuckled, amused by her persistence. "As it's written, *Where sin abounds, grace abounds all the more.*' Even if you've fallen ten thousand times, you've already been forgiven ten thousand times—and one more. This is why the story of the cross seems foolish to those blind to their sin. 'Why would someone need to suffer on my behalf?' they ask. But to those who have confronted their own heart and seen its corruption, the story of the cross becomes their only hope."

"The great accuser wants God's children to focus on their failures and unworthiness. He makes them doubt their inheritance and the promises God has made. He understands, better than any mortal, the precious gift of life. Lacking the authority to end mortal lives, he diminishes their earthly experience. He can cause you to stumble but cannot take away your salvation. He hates you for that. Even here, when he knows he's already lost your soul, he still accuses."

"Every breath and heartbeat of humanity glorifies God and sings His praises. Though you could not hear it with your human senses, we in the heavenly realm can hear the earth's song—and so can the accuser. And he despises it." The angel's voice was heavy with a deep exhale.

"What is the song of the earth?" Mom begged.

"Oh," he said as he looked up with closed eyes. "How I've missed it."

"It is the simple and fleeting moments that mortals so often overlook, yet they are cherished in eternity—the gentle breath of a slumbering child, the fiery rhythm of a heart overcome by love, the tears of a father as he beholds his newborn daughter, the tender embrace of a mother comforting her son. These are the melodies of life."

The angel turned his gaze toward Mom, his face grave yet radiant with purpose. "And then there are the lyrics—the measured wisdom imparted by a grandfather, the soothing hymn of a grandmother's presence, the uplifting words of a devoted teacher, the fearless rebuke of a righteous preacher, the sincere confession of a husband's remorse, the whispers of a wife's forgiveness, the playful jesting of a loyal friend, or the joyous laughter encircling a family table. These harmonies rise to the heavens, pleasing God.

"For God is the God of every moment, always finding delight in His creation. Not a single instance escapes His notice. Yet on earth, many fail to perceive this truth—that when they walk in love, live in grace, and breathe with compassion toward one another, it is then that heaven and earth collide."

Mom listened with her eyes closed and her hands clasped underneath her chin. A slight smile spread across her face as she visualized the distant memories.

"So the accuser has labored tirelessly to silence that song." The angel continued. "He prefers people live in the shadows of hell. They'll lose trust in their Creator if he can convince them to misunderstand God's love and faithfulness. That's why he sows chaos and then whispers, 'Look at what you've done,' 'You're a sinner,' 'You are worthless,' 'If people knew the real you, they'd see your ugliness,' 'You don't deserve grace.' He can diminish the power of peace and freedom by binding you with guilt and shame."

I marveled at how Mom had engaged the angel in such deep conversation. After a few awkward attempts those first few days after I arrived, I stopped trying, assuming they didn't speak if they didn't have to.

We were back on a familiar road, and I could barely contain my excitement. I held Mom's hand, pulling her along from just ahead. She snickered at my enthusiasm and reminded me that this was her journey through paradise, urging me to let her savor every moment. If she'd let me, I would have broken into a run, pulling her all the way to the gates.

Though the dense vegetation concealed what lay beyond, I knew we were nearing the gates. The sun's light had vanished, swallowed by the dazzling brilliance radiating from the city. Everything around us sparkled in a way that made me wonder if the grass, flowers, and leaves back home had always been so luminous, but only this all-encompassing light revealed their true brilliance. I imagined they did as the same divine architect crafted them.

Mom pointed out how the shadows on the mountain

faces and hillsides had vanished. Every crevice, overhang, and cave was bathed in light from every angle. Even the shade cast by the trees lining the stone road had disappeared. It felt as though we were wrapped in light, a mist of brilliance enveloping us.

Each of the many times I walked this road, guiding new arrivals to the gates, ignited an indescribable longing to enter the city with them and stay. But I had constantly been reminded of my instructions from that first day on the train—to await my mother. Today, that wait was over. The city seemed to draw every living thing toward itself with an irresistible pull, and now I could follow it. Like a bird intuitively knows where to migrate in the winter, so too is the soul of man, drawn towards heaven.

***

I recognized the opening in the trees where our road and thousands of others converging from every corner of paradise would merge into a vast, endless boulevard leading up to the gates.

Mom's head swiveled like an owl's as we stepped onto the white marble street, her eyes darting, soaking in the grandeur before her. No Caesar of Rome, pharaoh of Egypt, king of Babylon, prince of Persia, or czar of Russia could have conceived a more majestic entrance than this grand gateway, one of twelve that led into the city's outer gardens.

Pillars of solid pearl, towering like the redwoods in John's forest, lined each side of the boulevard. One would have to run for several minutes in either direction from the center to reach the edges of the wide marble street and the lush grass of the surrounding jungle. A canopy of silky, linen-like material stretched high above, flowing in the breeze like a white sea.

We were dwarfed by this portico, which seemed to have been designed for beings much larger than ourselves. Even if I had stood on the angel's shoulders, I wouldn't have reached the top of the golden base of each column. The thousand-mile road seamlessly cut through the jungle, as natural here as any tree, bush, or blade of grass.

We were still about a mile from the city's walls, but their sheer height made it feel as if we were right beneath them. Around us, hundreds of people bustled about, exchanging warm greetings, smiles, jokes, and laughter. Eventually, everyone made their way towards the gates. A woman attempted to corral a group of children darting and zigzagging across the dazzling white street. Several teenagers hurried past us, one of them holding a hand-drawn map while the others eagerly clustered around, pointing and twisting the map as they tried to orient themselves.

Two men walked alongside us in uniforms reminiscent of American soldiers from World War II. One was a fellow guide who clearly had waited for his friend much longer than I waited for Mom. Their laughter rang out as they chatted. The guide was young, perhaps twenty years old, with a thin, clean-shaven face and jet-black hair neatly combed back with a side part. The other looked to be in his eighties, heavier with bushy white brows and long gray hair that had turned white with age. They were two old buddies, once separated by the ravages of war and time, now joyfully reunited.

When Mom asked why there were so many elderly people around, I reminded her that they were as strong and healthy as oxen. They simply chose to keep their aged appearance because it was the season of life they cherished most. John had explained it to me when I first arrived.

"After all, what would heaven be without grandparents, Mom?" I nudged her playfully.

"Very true!" she agreed.

I glanced back at the road. It was perfectly straight, devoid of curves or dips, extending for miles until it vanished into the horizon. The white marble beneath our feet was flawless, a single continuous slab with no seams or splits.

The double gate was open wide, each panel at least ten

feet thick. The first time I saw it, the gate was closed, giving it the appearance of one solid, seamless barrier forming a grand, graceful arch. The panels were like melted translucent pearls, reflecting and refracting the surrounding light, the gold borders and hinges gleaming.

As we drew nearer, I gestured to the foundation of the walls, and Mom placed her palms over her heart, her eyes reflecting the pomp before us. She gazed up and down, side to side, absorbing every detail. Her wonder mirrored my own; I had never been this close to the walls. They had appeared solid gold from a distance, but up close, they were delicate and detailed, the work of a genius architect.

The foundation was made up of twelve layers, each roughly fifty feet high, and crafted from a different precious stone. I gestured to each layer, my finger tracing upward as I recited the names with pride.

"Jasper, sapphire, chalcedony, emerald, sardonyx, sardius, chrysolite, beryl, topaz, chrysoprase, jacinth, and amethyst!" The words rolled off my tongue, a little detail John had shared with me countless times.

Each layer shimmered in the light, a sort of mist of colors rising from the stones, creating a dazzling, ever-changing mosaic.

The walls above the foundation were crafted from translucent blue tanzanite, adorned with branching veins of gold that twisted like roots. Jewels, some unfamiliar to me, were embedded into the intricate designs. As I examined the patterns of gold and precious stones, I realized they were not random but rather a grand tapestry illustrating critical historical events and what I guessed were glimpses into the future. Were these walls, with their timeless artistry, a recording of both past and future long before any human had walked through the gates? Or maybe they changed along with the timeline of history? I wasn't sure.

When I turned to the left or right, the walls stretched as far as I could see. The first ten feet of the wall were crafted from gold bricks, each engraved with a name—there were millions, perhaps billions of them. I knew these were the names of the city's citizens, eternally etched into the golden frame. A thrill ran through me at the thought that Mom's and my names would be among those permanently inscribed on this magnificent wall.

Suddenly, a trumpet blast, similar to the one I'd heard when I first arrived on the train, shattered the tranquility, its sound emanating from within the walls and vibrating the marble beneath our feet. Cheers, and joyous screams erupted around us as everyone on the road and near the walls hurried toward the gates. Even the group of teenagers, their adventure forgotten, zoomed past us in a rush.

Then, we heard it. The music began as a gentle, rising melody, like the whisper of a breeze or the collective hum of countless voices in harmony. As the singing grew louder, it was accompanied by a crescendo of drums, violins, harps, flutes, tubas, trumpets, snares, and cymbals—a full choir and orchestra blending in a magnificent symphony. Though the words were distant and indistinct, the sound awakened all sorts of emotions deep within me. I wanted to cry or laugh, I wasn't sure.

We were desperate to join the throng surging toward the gates, but some great force held us back. Mom's eyes filled with desperation as she looked at me, and for once, I had no answers. This was as far as I had ever been.

"Anna. Luke." A booming voice cut through the clamor of the crowd.

# Seven

## *The Great Reunion*

The angel's eyes blazed with fire, his pupils like black holes capable of swallowing the entire universe. Mom and I instantly went numb. He was one of them—the gatekeepers I had seen before, departing the city on chariots.

Towering over us, he rested one hand on the pommel of his sword while the other held a massive scroll. Though there was no wind, his white tunic billowed, glowing, or perhaps burning with light—I couldn't tell. His fiery eyes were penetrating while the rest of his face was blurred.

Our feet felt fused to the marble beneath us as if we had become a permanent extension of the road—statues frozen in time. Mom's hand gripped mine, crushing my fingers in fear—or perhaps it was mine crushing hers.

Though his sandaled feet were firmly planted on the

road, the angel seemed weightless, more spirit than flesh, and yet he held absolute power over us. We couldn't move unless he willed it. I shuddered to think of the force he could unleash with his sword. His gaze alone was enough to keep us pinned in place like bugs beneath a crushing thumb. I silently pleaded for the angel accompanying us on our journey to intervene, but he was no longer by our side. Time felt meaningless under his power, every second stretching into eternity.

"Let me see the evidence upon you."

The words struck like lightning, and I couldn't tell if we heard them with our ears or if they pierced straight into our minds. His grip on the scroll slackened, and with a menacing snap, it unfurled, spilling down to the marble floor like a cascading waterfall of parchment. The scroll coiled over itself in endless folds until, at last, he pressed his hand on the chosen passage. Then, he began to read. Sparks flickered from the scroll, falling like embers to the ground as his finger swept left to right, revealing the hidden words.

Every moment of our lives was laid bare, with no deed, thought, or word left unspoken. As he read, we relived each one, helpless under the weight of his voice and the judgment of our actions.

My life unfolded before my eyes like a movie script brought vividly to life. It wasn't a linear timeline but a simultaneous cascade of memories like on the train when

I first arrived. Next to me, I couldn't tell what Mom was seeing or hearing, but in this reel of my life, I was both a child and an adult, seeing my whole life simultaneously as if I was peeking in through a window.

Whether I was ashamed or proud of it, big or small, every action and thought stood with equal significance. I could trace the ripple effect of every conversation, every word I uttered, how it made others feel, and what behaviors those feelings led to. My every decision and belief shaped the next series of events in ways I had never imagined. Nothing was left out: The brief moments of contentment, the endless repeated years of dissatisfaction, the long, quiet drives alone, the solitary lunches at work, the relentless self-criticism. Those small, seemingly insignificant passing moments filled the hours of my short and mostly unremarkable life. How desperately I wished I had been more present and intentional. Every second on Earth was indeed precious, yet I watched how I obsessively found ways to distract myself just to "get through" the days.

I saw the many paths my life could have taken—every possibility laid out before me. Somehow, I had managed to avoid or sabotage every reasonable opportunity.

It was painfully embarrassing to witness how, time after time, my fears guided my decisions and altered my future. So many great men had been placed in my path to fill the void left by my father: Police officers, football coaches, pastors, P.E. teachers—each had sympathized with me and tried to help. Yet, I refused to let go of my self-pity and bitterness. I kept everyone at a distance.

Thoughts I never imagined would be exposed were now being read aloud—the good, the bad, the ugly—all laid bare before me. It was excruciating.

In the same way, Mom's life was open before her. Her hand clutched mine tightly, but I was powerless to help her, just as she was powerless to save me. We stood together, yet alone, each of us held accountable for the paths we had walked, our choices, and the moments that had defined us.

"What evidence are you seeking?" I stammered. Did I say this aloud or think it? Either way, he heard me. After what I had just witnessed from the scroll, I knew he wouldn't find evidence of a life worthy of paradise.

Could Mom and I still enter? If we couldn't, wouldn't John have told us so? What if my name wasn't carved into the golden bricks after all? What if I had to stay in the countryside? Or worse... what if I deserved the pit? Every possibility crashed through my mind, and a fear I hadn't felt since before I came here overwhelmed me.

At least let Mom go in. She deserved it, didn't she?

All the while, people rushed past us, heading toward the concert beyond the gates. I desperately wanted to know why they weren't held back at the gate and could go in freely, but I knew that had nothing to do with me. I had to plead my case. Suddenly, I remembered the day I first arrived. "Jesus!" I shouted. "Jesus promised me I could come in when my mom joined me! He said, 'Soon you will be with me in paradise.' He said it!"

I could hear the desperation in my voice as I tried to convince the angel, but the truth was undeniable. The ugliness of my life far outweighed the good, and it was all too clear. My own life was testifying against me.

Then, the angel abruptly stopped reading. He turned the scroll so we could see what he saw. Next to each of our names was a brushstroke of blood.

"I wasn't looking for any good you've done," he thundered, tapping the scroll with his giant fingers. "I wouldn't find enough of that here. All who have sinned have fallen short of the glory of God. No one enters because of their works. Just as I once spared the homes of the captives in Egypt when I saw the blood of a lamb on their doorposts, in this age, I look for the same evidence upon each soul."

I remembered the biblical account of the Hebrews enslaved in Egypt. The angel of Death, apparently this one, was sent to strike down all the firstborn males in every household as a punishment against Pharaoh. The angel didn't check if the household belonged to Hebrews or Egyptians or whether they had done good deeds. He looked only for the blood of the lamb smeared on the doorposts and "passed over" that house. In that simple act of trust, all who followed God's instructions to Moses saved their households from this plague. From that moment on, it was known as the Passover Lamb—a symbol pointing to the final sacrificial lamb, which would come thousands of years later. In one ultimate act, this lamb would forever redeem anyone who trusted and believed.

"I have found what I was looking for!" he suddenly declared. An ear-deafening roar erupted from a crowd that had gathered just beyond the gates, out of our sight. Though visibly eager to reach their destination, all the people had stopped and waited for Mom and me. They cheered for us. I didn't recognize any of them, but their kind, smiling faces beamed, and they continued to wave us in. Our angel was there with them, waiting for us too.

Mom and I dashed through the gate as if the gatekeeper might change his mind. We weren't allowed in because we belonged to some exclusive club, were born into the right family, followed the right religion, or did enough of the right things. There was no list of accomplishments next to our names in the scroll that we could boast about. It wasn't because we were "good" or "decent" people. We entered the gates as deserving citizens, ready to accept our inheritance simply because of God's grace and the gift of the ultimate sacrifice.

All those teachings that once made little sense to an anxious, confused kid from D Street in South Boston became clear. I knew it, too. As a guide, I had helped calm others with that truth as I left them at the gate, but somehow, standing before the angel, holding our fate in his hands, my confidence wavered. The transcript of my life reminded me once again that if I were judged by my thoughts or deeds alone, I would be condemned.

As we approached the crowd, a swarm of children came running toward us—dozens of them. They surrounded Mom, and I lost my grip on her hand. The children tugged at her fingers and blouse, begging for her attention with gleeful laughter. They grabbed my hand, too, and swept us along, and soon, we were all running down the road together.

On this side of the gate, the road was made of solid gold, which was so pure it resembled crystal. A geology teacher once told me that gold, in its purest form, can be as transparent as glass. Of course, it would be abundant here. On earth, men killed and died for a nugget of gold; here, it formed the very fabric of the landscape.

As I ran with the children, I looked up past the valley of vineyards bordered by silver-leafed trees bearing golden fruit. I slowed to a stop, and Mom and her procession of children halted and turned back to me.

"Luke," she chuckled, still captivated by the children. "Are you coming?"

"Look," I said, pointing ahead. As Mom turned to follow my finger in the direction we were running, I saw her shoulders drop in disbelief. The golden road dipped along with the valley, but just past the vineyards lay a breathtaking sight.

Through a haze of brilliant light emerged the city's silhouette—not like any earthly city one sees from a distance, but something otherworldly. It seemed painted into the sky, like a mirage. This city was so vast and wide, and its buildings were so towering that it dominated the horizon even from miles away. Though we were far from the buildings, I had to look straight up to glimpse their tops. Unlike Earth's squared and mundane skyscrapers, these were uniquely designed, none resembling the other yet more harmonious and pleasing to the eye than any man-made structure. They reached skyward, where jumbo jets would fly if this were Earth. And high above the tops, red, purple, and bluish planets adorned the sky amidst billions of sparkling stars.

Deep within its parks and rivers, golden streets, and lush gardens teeming with animals, a light shone so brilliantly that it outshone the setting sun.

"We're home," Mom said, tears welling in her eyes.

"Yes, Mom, we're home," I replied.

As we resumed walking, I turned to the angel, who had caught up and was walking beside me. "Who are all these little ones? They won't leave her side."

"These are the children from the hospital," he said.

"The ones whose hands she held until their final breaths, as various sicknesses cut their lives short. Like you, they've been waiting for her for a long time!"

Mom overheard our conversation. She dropped to her knees, gently cupping each child's face and kissing them on their foreheads, one by one. The swarm of children grew even more excited and began to sing. They tugged her toward the city, and the angel and I followed behind, delighting in the joyful chaos.

As we neared the city, we approached a large black marble courtyard leading up to a brightly lit arena nestled among fields and vineyards—the golden road sliced directly through the middle, dividing it in two. The marble tiers of seats faced the road, making everything and everyone who traveled down it the center of attention. A sea of people had already gathered, filling the benches, while many more were rushing toward the arena. The source of the music and singing we had heard was clear now—something momentous was unfolding.

Suddenly, the sky dimmed as if someone had deliberately turned off the lights, revealing billions of stars that the city's overwhelming brilliance had hidden. Yet, an eternal light still glowed from somewhere at the city's center, casting a breathtaking backdrop of shadowy architecture, suspended bridges, and lush gardens behind the grand arena. God Himself was putting on a spectacular display.

The children began to shout excitedly. "Let's hurry, let's hurry! He's coming to greet you; he's coming!"

"Who's coming?" I heard Mom ask, but we were already running again. The closer we got to the arena, the more we were enveloped by a wave of pure joy and ecstasy reminiscent of our run through the forest. Mom and I raced each other, with her occasionally pulling ahead, only for me to catch up and surpass her. We were rushing towards the gathering.

When we reached the black marble courtyard, we pressed against the mob to get closer to the bleachers. The arena sparkled with torches of white flame, casting a dazzling light over the crowd. People were shouting, dancing, and embracing one another. Some were tightly wrapped together, spinning and tumbling to the ground in joyous heaps before pulling each other up and laughing. Others formed lines of twenty or more, kicking their feet and singing up at the star-filled night sky. I saw people climbing onto each other's shoulders, trying to glimpse whatever was unfolding on the road. Many others stood alone at the edges of the crowd, smiling, frequently wiping tears from their faces and periodically turning to wave us on, urging us to hurry.

"A lot of new arrivals today!" someone shouted as we pressed closer. Seeing thousands of people pointing towards the city, their excitement nearly palpable, I suddenly realized that many gathered here were also experiencing their first entry through the gates. This was our reception party.

As the music faded, a hush fell over the crowd. The steady thump of drums reverberated through our chests. A deafening roar erupted from those in the bleachers who had a clear view of what was happening up ahead. From our position at the back, we could only guess at the spectacle unfolding before us, but we saw a vibrant cascade of colors lighting up the faces in the sea of people. With flashing colors and musicians, a grand procession moved through the crowd of excited dancers.

The crowd had grown so large that it spilled out of the bleachers and onto the golden road. I stood on my toes and craned my neck, holding onto the shoulders of the man in front of me for a better view, and relayed everything I could see to Mom.

At the forefront of the procession marched what had to be ten thousand drummers clad in snow-white flowing pants, their rhythmic beats setting the tone for the celebration. Their powerful, synchronized drumming resonated through the open arena like peals of thunder. The deep, resonant thuds of the large drums blended with the sharp, rapid strikes of the smaller hand-held drums, creating a beat we felt in our bones as much as we heard. They stomped in perfect unison, their sparkling gold sandals, bracelets, armbands, and headbands glinting in the light.

Behind the drummers, two columns of musicians with

trumpets, flutes, and cymbals enriched the procession with a vibrant melody. The trumpets' bold, brassy calls heralded the arrival, while the flutes wove a lighter, intricate harmony around the dominant drumbeat.

The excitement among the gathered crowd surged as they pushed closer to the front, still leaving ample space for the horses and chariots of warrior angels that followed the musicians. Amid the dancing and singing, the angels, though imposing, seemed less intimidating, their faces stern but their eyes sharp and probing.

Thousands of dancers twirled alongside the musicians, perfectly synchronizing with the rhythm. Each step they took sent a whoosh through the air as their gliding feet brushed against the golden road like a powerful gust of wind. Adorned in flowing, brightly colored garments, they spun, leaped, and flashed radiant smiles, their gestures both graceful and commanding. The dance embodied the music's energy.

Trailing behind was a grand, ornate chariot drawn by seven majestic white horses, their shoulder height taller than two men standing on each other. The lead horse was adorned with a golden battle mask, revealing only its eyes, ears, and muzzle. Its mane seemed ablaze, directing the procession.

Then I saw him. The King of Kings stood on the chariot, draped in robes adorned with jewels that sparkled with every subtle movement. He was enveloped in radiant light, just like when I first saw him on the train. His brilliance was so intense that his face remained hidden from view.

In our shared exhilaration, we leaped with joy, embracing strangers who hugged us in return. Amidst the celebration, a chant emerged from the crowd, spreading like a wave until it engulfed us all.

"Oh, the cross! What have you done? You have already won!" Mom and I shouted, along with the multitude, from the top of our lungs. Then, a deep, authoritative voice resonated through the noise, causing the chants to fade into a hush.

"Behold the Lamb of God who takes away the sins of the world! He is the King of Righteousness, the King of Heaven and Earth, the King of Glory, the King of Ages! The King of Past, Present, and Future, the Beginning and the End! The Builder of Galaxies, the Composer of the Universe, the Creator of All Living Things! The Breath of Life, the Everlasting, the Magnificent, the Merciful, the Patient! The Perfect Lamb, the Beginning of Wisdom, the Source of Joy, the Epitome of Perfection! The Scales of Justice, the Prince of Peace, the Definition of Might, the Provider for the Poor, the Healer of the Sick, the Great Shepherd! The Light of the World, the Comforter, Protector, the Author of Love! Emanuel…"

"Mom, it's John!" I shouted, lifting her by the waist to get a better view. John ran up and down the procession like a whirlwind, shouting and pointing excitedly at Jesus on the chariot.

"What a job he's got," I laughed. "Even here, he's announcing Jesus' arrival. I'd recognize that voice anywhere!"

An ear-splitting roar erupted from the thousands in response to John. The sound crashed against the arena and echoed through the towering city in the distance like waves relentlessly pounding against a cliff. The crowd surged as one, a tidal wave of adoration, acknowledging the presence of the source of all life among us. This was how it was always meant to be, even on Earth—Creator and creation united. In Him, we lived, moved, and had our being.

Standing among those who were once strangers from distant lands and varied backgrounds, I saw our oneness. We were liberated from the need to clothe ourselves in titles, deeds, or accomplishments and the constant need for validation and acceptance. The people around me had become more precious than family. The command to "love your neighbor as yourself" suddenly felt simple and natural. How had we missed this truth on Earth? A profound, indescribable love for every soul around me surged with every heartbeat, and I felt their love return to me.

Suddenly, the grand parade stopped as Jesus descended from his chariot. He shed his robes and draped them over the back of a white horse. Clad in a simple white tunic secured by a worn leather belt, he resembled the image I had long imagined of him walking the ancient roads of Galilee, Samaria, and Judea. He embraced the crowd one by one, pulling each person into a tight, uplifting hug. Children, elders, and young men alike were lifted from their feet, enveloped in the profound warmth of his embrace.

I watched as he drew nearer to where Mom and I stood. The children, still clustered around her, erupted in excited shouts and frantic waves, urging Jesus to look our way. They leaped and pointed at Mom, their enthusiasm spilling out.

When his gaze finally found us, a smile spread across his face. Even through the surrounding brilliance, I could feel the warmth of his expression. As if sensing his purpose, the crowd in front of us parted, creating a path through which he moved with effortless grace. My legs felt weak with each step he took closer to us.

And then, there he was, standing right before us. At that moment, I was torn between falling to my knees in reverence and throwing my arms around him in sheer joy. I felt insignificant and profoundly cherished in his presence, as if I were nothing more than a speck of dust yet valued beyond measure.

"Luke, Anna!" His voice was gentle, balancing firmness with undeniable warmth. Just like our first encounter on the train, I found myself unraveling. I dropped to my knees, pressing my forehead against the cool, gleaming marble of the arena floor. Mom was sobbing quietly beside me, her trembling fingers resting on my back.

"Come," he said softly. "There will be plenty of time for worship and celebration when I sit beside my Father on the throne. For now, just say hello. I've been waiting for you both." I heard a soft chuckle in his voice.

His words were simple and direct, as I had expected. After all, he was the same carpenter who had walked among us, understanding our deepest needs and struggles. I rose to my feet, my eyes meeting his. Mom was already in his embrace. The light was now gentler, and I could see his compassionate brown eyes gazing at me. He extended his hand, inviting me to join him and Mom in a heartfelt embrace.

How could this be? I wondered. How was I worthy of such a moment? To be known by name, to be awaited by the Son of God—how could this be? In his embrace, everything felt perfectly right.

"I have a special task for you both in my kingdom," he said with a warm smile, slightly pulling back to meet our eyes. He brushed the tears from Mom's face and gently lifted her chin.

"Since you love the little ones so much, just as I do,

you will become a mother to many here, Anna. Few have the capacity to care for them as you do. Will you accept this role?"

"Yes! Yes! Yes!" Mom exclaimed through her tears. "Nothing would make me happier."

Jesus chuckled, his eyes twinkling. "Very well then," he said, still smiling. "Luke, will you assist your mother?" He asked, turning to me.

I couldn't choke out any words but managed to nod. He acknowledged my response, and then his expression brightened as if he had just remembered something.

"Oh, there is someone I'd like you to meet."

He turned and glanced over his shoulder, past the sea of smiling and eager faces, towards his chariot. With a wave, we saw a small figure leap from the chariot and race towards us.

As the little girl ran in our direction, Jesus gently let go of Mom's hand, continuing to embrace others amidst the crowd.

"Mom!" The child's voice rang out, filled with excitement. "Mom!" The crowd buzzed with renewed energy. We strained to keep our eyes on her as she wove through the sea of people. Was she calling my mother? Mom and I craned our necks, trying to catch a glimpse through the swirling mass of waving and dancing figures.

"Mom!" The voice rang out again as the girl pushed through the crowd. Finally, she squeezed her way to the front and stood directly before Mom, gazing up at her with wide, round eyes.

She had a round, chubby face with rosy cheeks and a tiny nose. Her light brown hair was parted down the middle and styled into two pigtails that bounced with every step. She wore a yellow sleeveless sundress adorned with white polka dots and black closed-toe sandals over white socks. The diamond bracelet on her left wrist sparkled as she lifted her hands, reaching for Mom.

Mom and I exchanged bewildered glances. Was she mistaking Mom for someone else? Mom hesitated momentarily before gently clasping the little girl's hands in her own.

"Mom," the child said again, her voice filled with anticipation. "I've been waiting to meet you."

"I...I'm sorry," Mom stammered, her voice trembling. "I'm not sure you have the right person. What is your name?"

"Leyla," she replied, her eyes wide and earnest. "That's the name I chose. You didn't give me a name."

Mom's hands flew to her mouth. "Could it be?" she whispered, her voice barely audible. "My miscarriage?"

Leyla nodded, her big eyes crinkling at the corners as

she offered Mom a gentle, approving smile.

"Before me or after me?" I mouthed to Mom as Leyla tugged her through the crowd. I stood in stunned silence, grappling with the reality that I now had a little—or rather, big—sister.

"Long before you," Leyla said, pausing and turning to look at me. I was astonished that she had heard me, but then again, this was heaven, so perhaps it made sense. Mom gently wiped tears from her eyes and lovingly smoothed Leyla's pigtails.

"I'm your little brother, Luke," I shouted above the noise.

"I know," Leyla replied with a smile, tossing her head to shift her pigtails out of her face. "I love you, little brother." She stood on her tiptoes and pressed a tender kiss to my cheek.

"Were you here all along?" I asked, bewildered. "In the city? I… I was waiting for Mom in the country."

"I know," she said with a matter-of-fact tone. "Jesus told me you were here." She removed the bracelet from her wrist and carefully slipped it onto mine. "I made this for you the day you arrived."

Leyla grabbed my hand with excitement. "I've already picked a place for us to live," she said. "It's in a little village right next to the city. It's like the kind of house you and Mom always dreamed of moving to. Our house has gardens with flowers," she added, her eyes sparkling, "and it's got golden brick pathways. It's the most beautiful and cozy place you've ever seen. I know you'll love it."

"Come on," she urged. "I have so much to show you!"

The End

# God's Promises
## (Bible verses referenced in this book)

"For God so loved the world, that he gave his only Son, that whoever believes in him should not perish but have eternal life." (John 3:16)

"Now faith is confidence in what we hope for and assurance about what we do not see. (Hebrews 11:1)

"The Lord is close to the brokenhearted and saves those who are crushed in spirit." (Psalm 34:18)

"He will take our weak mortal bodies and change them into glorious bodies like his own, using the same power with which he will bring everything under his control." (Philippians 3:21)

"But he was pierced for our transgressions, he was crushed for our iniquities; the punishment that brought us peace was on him, and by his wounds we are healed." (Isaiah 53:5)

"I am a voice shouting in the wilderness, 'Clear the way for the LORD's coming!'" (John 1:23)

"I will give you the keys of the kingdom of heaven; whatever you bind on earth will be bound in heaven, and whatever you loose on earth will be loosed in heaven." (Matthew 16:19)

"Truly, I say to you, among those born of women, there has arisen no one greater than John the Baptist. Yet the one who is least in the kingdom of heaven is greater than he." (Matthew 11:11)

"The greatest among you will be your servant." (Matthew 23:11)

"He has planted eternity in the human heart, but even so, people cannot see the whole scope of God's work from beginning to end. (Ecclesiastes 3:11)

"Let anyone who is thirsty come to me and drink. Whoever believes in me, as Scripture has said, rivers of living water will flow from within them." (John 7: 37-39)

"And he showed me a river of water of life, bright as crystal, proceeding out of the throne of God and of the Lamb, in the middle of its wide road" (Revelation 22:1)

"However, when the Son of Man comes, will he find faith on the earth?" (Luke 18:8)

"So if the Son sets you free, you will be free indeed." (John 8:36)

"Let anyone who is thirsty come to me and drink. Whoever believes in me, as Scripture has said, rivers of living water will flow from within them." (John 7:37-39)

"Whoever drinks of this water will be thirsty again, but whoever drinks of the water that I will give him will never be thirsty again." (John 4:13-14)

"Where sin abounds, grace abounds more" (Romans 5:20)

"Therefore, I tell you, her many sins have been forgiven—as her great love has shown. But whoever has been forgiven little loves little." (Luke 7:47)

"Jesus said to him, 'I am the way, and the truth, and the life. No one comes to the Father except through me." (John 14:6)

"Very truly I tell you, whoever hears my word and believes him who sent me has eternal life and will not be judged but has crossed over from death to life." (John 5:24)

"Therefore, there is now no condemnation for those who are in Christ Jesus." (Romans 8:1)

"Come to me, all you who are weary and burdened, and I will give you rest." (Matthew 11:28)

"The God who made the world and everything in it is

the Lord of heaven and earth and does not live in temples built by human hands. And he is not served by human hands, as if he needed anything. Rather, he himself gives everyone life and breath and everything else. From one man he made all the nations, that they should inhabit the whole earth; and he marked out their appointed times in history and the boundaries of their lands. God did this so that they would seek him and perhaps reach out for him and find him, though he is not far from any one of us. "For in him we live and move and have our being." (Acts 17:24-28)

"For if you forgive other people when they sin against you, your heavenly Father will also forgive you." (Matthew 6:14)

## About the Author

Michael is a motivational speaker and best-selling author who has impacted millions of people with his message of resilience.

From students, to athletes, to leaders, to business professionals, Michael motivates audiences to take personal responsibility for their lives, reconnect to their purpose, and cultivate success in every aspect of their lives. As a child, he immigrated to the United States just before the collapse of the Soviet Union and the end of the Cold War and is the grandson of a 'Siege of Leningrad' and Dachau camp survivor. Michael's talent for story-telling and his success principles motivate and empower audiences to smash fears, limitations, and passive, excuse-oriented mindsets. He reveals how the personal choices we make, the attitudes we carry, and the principles we choose to live by, determine the success & quality of our lives.

If you would like to have Michael speak at your event, please visit Michael's website here:

## WWW.SPEAKLIFE365.COM

Be sure to find Michael's other books:

## *The Mount of Olives:*
## *11 Declarations to an Extraordinary Life*

Combining courage, faith, wisdom and wonder into an inspiring tale of self-discovery, The Mount of Olives takes readers for an emotional ride through the life of a boy whose search for better becomes a discovery of something extraordinary. Michael Ivanov's masterpiece tells the story of Felix, the Roman boy who despite all opposition, yearns to gain a worldly treasure. His journey will lead him to riches far different—and far more satisfying—than he ever imagined. Felix's quest teaches us the essential wisdom of listening to our hearts, recognizing opportunity and learning the golden principles strewn along life's path, and, most importantly, to follow our dreams.

## *The Traveler's Secret:*
## *Ancient Proverbs for Better Living*

The Traveler's Secret offers an ancient story of one man's choices—and the principles that make the difference between failure and success. In this fable about following dreams, Michael V. Ivanov's latest masterpiece reveals the journey of Agisillus, a vagabond in ancient Gaul, and his extraordinary encounter with a mysterious traveler. This book reveals secrets to living an extraordinary and purposeful life, amassing personal wealth, and leaving a legacy that continues to sow seeds of life into the world. It shares the ancient proverbs of the wise and the foolish and teaches the universal laws of prosperity. Author Michael V. Ivanov provides concrete advice for living a wise and purposeful life.

## *The Servant With One Talent: Five Success Principles from the Greatest Parable Ever Told*

To bring your dreams and desires to fulfillment, you must invest in your talents. This book shows you how to become successful and live with purpose by sharing the secrets hidden in an ancient parable, which holds the universal laws of prosperity.

The Servant With One Talent is an instant classic that holds the key to all you desire and everything you wish to accomplish. Through the story of the unprofitable and lazy servant in ancient Babylon, Michael V. Ivanov provides a unique perspective on the classic parable of the talents. This book provides concrete advice for creating a successful and purposeful life while fulfilling your destiny and becoming the person you were created to be. While many people are burying their dreams, talents, skills and abilities in the desert, like the unprofitable servant did at the beginning of this story, the successful are investing into their skills, talents, and abilities.

## *The Cabin at the End of the Train: A Story About Pursuing Dreams*

From a chance meeting with a remarkable old man by the name of "Carl," a mysterious WWII veteran who shows up on the train at just the right time, The Cabin at the End of the Train provides 12 priceless lessons about purpose, life, and the importance of perspectives.

**Get signed copies of all of Michael's books at
WWW.MOUNTOFOLIVESBOOK.COM**

Made in the USA
Columbia, SC
31 January 2025